Arianna Snow's Prequel Series:

The Lochmoor Glen Series

"Patience, My Dear is an enthralling, well crafted, superbly written 'page-turner' of a read, fruitfully exposed to the impairing remembrance and encounter of a first young love when nearing mid-life many years later. *Patience, My Dear* is very strongly recommended for readers searching for a superbly authored telling of an intricate and entertaining tale involving a love consumed memory and an ever-deepening mystery."

"A comedy of errors held together with taut suspense and biting dialogue, *My Magic Square* is a delicious pleasure from beginning to end."

"Unwelcome visitors make their residence nearby, and there's a reason why they're unwelcome. *Threaded Needles* follows two amateur detectives whose bond of blood is unbreakable as they try to find out just what suspicious character Ian MacGill and his associate are planning. The resulting adventure is entertaining and enthralling. *Threaded Needles* is highly recommended for community library mystery collections."

"A compelling human drama unfolds, making *Blessed Petals* a very solidly recommended read."

"Without a Sword is another entry into the Lochmoor Glen series, and does the series justice."

"Another exciting thriller from Arianna Snow, *Kade* is not a read to be missed for fans of the series."

"A gripping read of drama, *Please, Tell Me* is a top pick and very highly recommended."

"Geoffrey's Secret is a must for lovers of historical fiction and the flavor of the 1800s."

"For those who have enjoyed the previous entries into the series or dramas surrounding socialites, *Each Rising Tide* is a fine pick, not to be overlooked." **—Midwest Book Review**

Heated Exchange

A NOVEL

Arianna Snow

Golden Horse Ltd.
Davis City, Iowa

An Original Publication of Golden Horse Ltd.
Davis, IA 50065 U.S.A.

www.ariannaghnovels.com
ISBN 13: 9781513617909

Library of Congress Control Number: 2016961882
First Printing
Volume 1 of the *Beyond Lochmoor Glen Series*

Printed and bound in the United States of America
by Publishers' Graphics, LLC, Carol Stream, IL

Cover: Arianna Snow's photograph
Printed by White Oak Promotional Products, Lancaster PA

In loving memory
of
my father's beloved brother,
Uncle Sam,
and his grandson,
Robert Jr.

A special Good-Bye-for-Now to our sweet lab puppy,
Patience Halo
(Honey Baby I Love You)

My Special thanks to :
GOD

KAEZA
(editorial work and encouragement)

David,
family and friends
(support)

Momma and Daddy
(packaging)

David Miller
(cover production supervision)

HIRAM GEOFFREY MCDONNALLY

FAMILY TREE

FATHER CAPTAIN GEOFFREY LACHLAN MCDONNALLY

HALF-BROTHER GUILLAUME ZIGMANN MCDONNALLY

ADOPTIVE MOTHER: ELOISE ZIGMANN

WIFE: TRINA DUNMORE MCDONNALLY

CHILDREN: GRAHAM, ROYSTON

and VERA   MCDONNALLY

MOTHER AMANDA SELRACH MCDONNALLY

SISTER HANNAH RUTH MCDONNALLY

NIECE SOPHIA RUTH SIERZIK

HUSBAND: RAHZVON MANSTRONG SIERZIK

CHILDREN: ZANYA, VONMANSTRONG, RUTHIA

and IVY SIERZIK

WIFE LIVIA NICHOLS MCDONNALLY

ADOPTED SON THOMAS "KADE" MCDONNALLY

TWINS AMANDA and ALEXANDER MCDONNALLY

UNCLE EDWARD CALEB MCDONNALLY

NAOMI BEATRICE

(MACKENZIE) MCDONNALLY

FAMILY TREE

FATHER NATHAN ELIAS MACKENZIE

BROTHER JEREMIAH JAMES MACKENZIE

MOTHER BEATRICE SMITHFIELD MACKENZIE

FIANCE: DANIEL O'LEARDON

HALF-BROTHER HENRY STRICKLAND (SON of CECIL)

WIFE: PEARL STRICKLAND

NEPHEWS MARVIN and CONRAD STRICKLAND

HUSBAND EDWARD CALEB MCDONNALLY

ADOPTED DAUGHTER ALLISON S. O'CONNOR MONROE

HUSBAND: ADAM MONROE SR,

GRANDCHILDREN ADDISON BEATRICE MONROE

ADAM MONROE JR.

DAUGHTER LUCIA SMITHFIELD MCDONNALLY "SMITTY"

FRIENDS

HARRIET DUGAN

    ADOPTED SON: HENRY MCTAVISH "TAVY"

    WIFE: MERCEDES M, STOCKDALE MCTAVISH

    ADOPTED SON: RUFUS MCTAVISH

    DAUGHTER: PHEMIA MERCEDES MCTAVISH

MARYANNE and BRUCE WHEATON

    DAUGHTERS: WILMOTH, MARVEL, CORINNE,

        JEANIE, DARA and MARTHA

    SON: BRUCE WHEATON JR.

AGNES and JAKE KILVERT

    DAUGHTER: BERYL KILVERT

    SON: GAVIN KILVERT

MILES (MCDONNALLY MANOR BUTLER)

JULES (BRACHNEY HALL BUTLER)

The Chapters

Chapter 1

"Von's Secret"

"Deed in unfathomable mines,
Of never failing skill,
He treasures up his bright designs,
And works his sov'reign will."

—William Cowper

It was March of 1932; fourteen years had passed since the end of the Great War. The population of Lochmoor Glen, Scotland had transformed with the arrival of several new faces, and many residents having moved on to settle in other parts of the world.

Ruthia Sierzik, one of Sophia and Rahzvon's triplets, bound up the stairs of the McDonnally mansion and flew into her sister, Zanya's room. Ruthia, her siblings, and their parents had relocated into the east wing of Sophia's Uncle's home, after Rahzvon lost most of his investments in the Wall Street crash of 1929.

"Zonnie, what on earth are you doing? We have less than one-half hour before the guests will be arriving! Look at your hair! You're not even dressed, yet!"

"Ruthie, could you please save the lectures for someone who cares. I need to finish this page of my manuscript; I'm at a crucial point." Her pen moved swiftly across the page.

"Write, write, write! Do you do anything else?" She yanked the tablet from her sister's hand. "Put that down and sit up straight, so I can style your hair." She ran the comb back through the sides of her sister's hair.

"My hair is fine."

"Pish, posh! You're wearing it like mine. We *are* triplets, after all." She began brushing the shoulder length strands.

"Are you insisting that Von, wear his hair in one of those sparkly nets, too? After all, he *is* one of the triplets," Zanya said and snickered.

"Aren't you a barrel of laughs? And it's called a snood and it is very sophisticated."

"I'm not the sophisticated type."

"Tonight, you will be. Now hold still while I pin up the sides." After strategically placing several hairpins in Zanya's hair locks, Ruthia spun Zanya around. "Now, for the face."

"What's *wrong* with it? The dear Lord created it."

"This is no time to get pious on me. Does it look like mine?"

"Heaven's no! Yours is painted up like a—"

"Never mind. Get with the times—everyone uses face cosmetics, now."

"Mother doesn't."

"Mother is beautiful without them. Besides, she is old and Father would throw a royal tantrum, if she did. Wait here while I get my beauty case...and don't touch your hair!"

"*Beauty case*," Zanya sighed, wrinkling her nose and turning to the mirror. "Such a fuss—I think that I look just fine."

The truth of the matter was that Ruthia knew that Zanya's face was in no need of improvement. She was the spitting image of their mother at their age. However, Ruthia would never openly acknowledge it and covered for her true feelings by insisting on giving her sister a supposed *necessary* makeover. Why did Zanya have the gorgeous black, McDonnally locks, while her hair was straight and a boring brown? Why did Zanya have the tiny feet while she wore "huge" special ordered shoes? Yes, and then there was their father's annoying nickname for her mother "Little One" and to Zanya, "Littlest One." Who was Ruthia? The "Giant One"?

Ruthia quickly returned to her sister's room, toting her cosmetic case. She sat the pink celluloid box on the vanity and lifted the lid.

Zanya peered inside. "Really, Ruthie, this is obscene. You must have spent a small fortune on all of this."

"Keep quiet, watch and learn. We'll start with the eyes and work our way down." Ruthia dabbed a small brush in the eyeshadow.

"Down to where? You are *not* painting my toenails!"

"Not this time—only because you're wearing closed-toe heels. Now hold still." She placed a palm on Zanya's forehead and gently leaned Zanya's head back.

"What are you planning to do to my eyes?"

"I'm going to give you that doll-like look. Now, hush."

"I may be smaller, but I'm not a doll; I'm a real girl!" she objected.

Why was Zanya always whining about being small? Ruthia should only be so lucky.

"Correction, Zonnie—*woman*. Get used to the idea. You are seventeen today, need I remind you? Hold still." Ruthia applied the soft brown eyeshadow. "This makes your eyes look deep-set."

Zanya frowned at her reflection. "They look like yours," she grumbled. "Ghastly."

"Sultry—not ghastly. Now, for the lashes. Don't move or you'll have mascara everywhere and look like a panda."

"Ruthie, I—"

"Oh, hush! I'm an artist at work. Be grateful that we were blessed with two parents who gave us thick, long lashes, otherwise we'd be like poor Smitty."

"What's wrong with Smitty?"

"Our unfortunate cousin inherited Uncle Edward's piddly, thin eyelashes—not the McDonnally lashes. Poor girl will probably have to spend half her life in the salon having fake lashes applied."

"I never noticed her la—not the curler, Ruthie!" Zanya exclaimed in what could only be described as pure horror.

"Very well." Ruthia dropped the curler into the case. "I suppose yours will do. Now for the cheeks." She rummaged through the disarray of tubes and jars. She finally located the rouge. "Have you heard who's coming?" she asked, opening a jar.

"Everyone in the village."

"No, I mean *who*—as in Rufus McTavish,"

she announced, smiling.

"Oh? I thought he and Tavy were still out to sea."

"No. I overheard his grandmother telling Eloise that he would be here tonight. Of course, I knew that he would dare not miss my seventeenth birthday celebration." Ruthia grinned, dabbing the mauve rouge on her sister's cheeks.

Zanya rolled her eyes upward. *"Our* seventeenth birthday." She looked up. "How long has he been gone, Ruthie?"

"Four *long* years. Hold perfectly still and keep your lips together. I need to shape them like a cupid bow for that pouty look." She stepped back and squinted at her sister's reflection. "You're tolerable. Look." Ruthia pointed towards the mirror.

"Pouty? I'm not unhappy about today—we are having a party." She glanced into the mirror and up at her sister's glare. "What's the matter, failed in your artistic talents?" Zanya teased.

"No, nothing's wrong. You had better get dressed." Ruthia started to leave and looked back at her sister. The cosmetics only enhanced Zanya's natural beauty. Zanya was a McDonnally, through and through. Ruthia, on the other hand, took after her father, Rahzvon's side. He was certainly handsome enough, but Ruthia favored his mother—and nothing was *ever* mentioned about *her* extraordinary beauty. Zanya's petite frame did not help matters; Ruthia was said to have come from good Kosdrevian stock—noted farm women. Quite a turn of events, as Ruthia had started out as the "runt of the litter" as Harriet Dugan had tagged her.

With a quick shake of her head, Ruthia returned to her room and tossed the case on the bed. *I have to focus on fashion. It is my only saving grace.* She faced the facts; she was another Mercy Stockdale. *However*, she reconsidered, *Mercy ended up with the handsome Tavy.* "Although...her countenance is more feminine than mine," she muttered.

Ruthia slid the dirty laundry from her vanity bench and plopped down in front of the mirror. She stared at the image before her, remembering the haunting phrases from the village community: "Look at wee Zanya and her tiny frocks!" "She's so petite! Such a darling!"

Did anyone ever compliment *her*? The horrid words screamed in her head, "Why is Ruthia so much larger? She started out smaller. Guess she likes to eat!" And then the sickening laughter inevitably followed.

Yes, she, like her mother Sophia, liked to eat, but that was not the reason for her Kosdrevian features!

With her elbows resting on the vanity top, she held her face in her hands and closed her eyes. The only time that she felt small and "petite" was in the presence of her hero—her great Uncle Hiram. He was everything thing that she admired: big, powerful, uncommonly handsome, intelligent, wealthy and most importantly—he *alone* understood her.

She recalled that while the church congregation was doting on precious Zanya, Uncle Hiram would scoop her up and take her out to the churchyard where they would walk about conversing, ignoring everyone.

He made her feel like the most important person in the world. *He still listens to me.*

Her eyelids flew open to examine the room that was the complete visual opposite of Zanya's immaculate bedroom.

"She spends entirely too much time in her room organizing and writing," she mumbled.

Her sense of duty called, *I'd better check on Von.* "Von, Von!" Ruthia yelled, marching down the hall.

"Ruthia, tone it down."

She turned around to Rahzvon. "Sorry, Father, but everyone's behind schedule."

"I'm not."

"Oh, Father, it takes little effort on your part. You're as handsome as the day that I met you."

"Yes, and I'm certain that you have a crystal clear memory of that second when we met, seventeen years ago," he laughed.

"I do...a little one."

He looked both ways down the hall.

"Where *is* your brother?"

"I don't know, but he had better be dressed by now and prepared to meet the guests. I finally got Zanya in ship shape."

"Ruthia, you should be a drill sergeant."

"I could never be so horridly masculine. I'm just very well organized," she stated primly.

"Eloise could use you when she breaks in the new housekeeper."

Ruthia's eyes widened. "*New* house-keeper?"

"Yes, Hiram is retiring Mrs. Zigmann."

"Oh, no, what will the poor dear do all day?"

"I hear that she's planning on moving to London to live near Guillaume, Trina and the grandchildren."

"She can't go! I have known her forever! How will I get on without her? She has always been there to help me!" she panicked.

"*Her* happiness is what counts, Ruthia. Things change, now concentrate on the party. Have you seen your sister, Ivy?"

"No—both my siblings are AWOL," she mumbled.

"I need to find them. Your mother wants to check Von's tie and Ivy's hair."

"Father, she is *thirteen*—why don't you let Ivy get her hair cut—at least to shoulder length?"

"Because her two older sisters did! Now,

go and wash that paint off your face."

From behind them, Sophia cut in, "Leave it, Ruthie." She turned to her husband. "Rahzie all of the young ladies use cosmetics."

"Thank you, Mother," Ruthia said, grinning. Rahzvon let out a sigh of frustration and left.

Sophia looked down the hall. "Ruthia, have you seen Von and Ivy?"

"No, Mama, I am going for my shoes. I am surrounded by dawdlers," she muttered. Ruthia felt that she should have been born first. She was the authority figure. Zanya and Von lacked the innovation and inspiration to get anything done in a timely fashion, in her opinion.

Sophia headed towards Ivy's room. Ruthia returned to her room, picked up her very large shoes, and regarded them with contempt.

Von was sitting at his desk.

"Vonnie, it's beautiful!" his younger sister declared.

"Thank you, Ivy, but please call me Von—I *am* seventeen, now." He held the sketch up and examined it. "Do you think Trina would wear this? She's the most sophisticated woman who I know."

"Trina? Don't let Mother hear you say that, but, yes, she would look smashing in it. Where do you get these ideas, Vonnie...I mean Von, magazines?"

"No, little sister, they are all up here," he replied, tapping his forehead with his index finger.

Ivy was Von's greatest fan. Her big brother could do no wrong, but she was quiet frank and honest in her opinions. Von trusted her judgment but had been striving to teach her the virtue of tact since the day she had voiced her negative opinion of the minister's outlandish tie at a church picnic. Ivy, although only thirteen, had a good eye for color and symmetry. Von secretly hoped that she would join him in his love of fashion design, but Ivy made no mention of becoming an artist in any regard.

"Would you design a frock for me, Vonnie?"

"*Von*, Ivy, please. I am partial to clothing for adult women, but for you, I'll give it a shot." He pointed a warning finger at her. "Ivy, you *have* kept my designing a secret?"

"Yes, Vonnie, er, *Von*, only *I* am privileged to know of your incredible artistic talent, but when are you planning to tell Mama and Daddy? What about their plans for you?"

Yes, what about their plans for him? He cringed at the thought of their reactions. Telling them would be an incredibly difficult task and he dreaded it.

"Don't worry, Ivy, I'll tell them very soon. I can't avoid it too much longer. A London designer has asked to mentor me."

"You'll be leaving me? No, Vonnie!" she panicked, hugging him. He removed her hands from his neck and took them in his.

"My sweet Ivy, we'll write to each other and you knew that I was originally going to London to work in Guillaume's firm, anyway. You knew that," he said gently.

"But I thought that with your fashion career, you could stay in Lochmoor Glen."

"There's no future in fashion here."

She looked downcast. "Won't it be expensive...to live there?"

"I'll need only room and board." He smiled briefly.

She embraced him. "I'll miss you so much."

He hugged her in return. "You can come to visit. Besides, you wanted to visit Vera in Town, didn't you?" Vera, Guillaume and Trina's daughter, was now nine and studying to be a ballerina, like her mother.

"Yes, I do!" Ivy's eyes brightened.

"When you visit, she might teach you some dance steps," he said, smiling.

"She taught me the positions when she visited the last time."

Von watched as she glanced at her moving feet and explained, "Watch. First position, second position—"

A pert bellow interrupted them, "Von! Ivy!" Sophia's voice echoed down the hall.

Ivy looked toward the door. "We'd better

get moving—Mama's on the warpath!"

"Remember, my designing is *our* secret, for now."

"I cross my heart," she promised, gesturing.

"There you are!" Sophia muttered from the doorway. "Von, come here and let me fix your tie. Ivy don't move."

"Do you want to stand on the bed, Mother?" Von laughed, discreetly scooting his drawing pad under the coverlet.

"I am not *that* short." She straightened the tie and glared up at her son.

"You're shorter than Ruthia."

"She takes after your father."

"I guess you're still taller than Zanya," Von pointed out. *Zanya.* Why couldn't he be more like her? She knew what she wanted. She spoke her mind and was firm in her beliefs.

"Hold still, so that I can tie this," Sophia said, adjusting the lengths of the tie ends.

"Mama, you're taller than me," Ivy chimed in.

"Yes, dear, I am thrilled to be taller than my thirteen-year-old daughter by one-half inch. There, Von. Now, get upstairs, to the ballroom; the guests are arriving. Come with me, Ivy—I need to tie in your hair ribbon." She snatched the hand of her youngest and whisked her off to Ivy's bedroom.

Von paused by the bed. Yes, how would his parents take the news of his abandonment of the architectural career? His father would never understand. Being the only son, Von had hoped to form an alliance with his father, but it had never happened. His father was very much a loner and was forever disapproving of his son's small failures—Von was not living up to Rahzvon's middle name, Manstrong. Although lacking his father's strength, Von did his best to share his father's better character traits: his kindness and generosity. But Von could be as tenacious as his father who was hell-bent on his son becoming an architect. No, this change in plans would not be well-accepted, to say the least. Why couldn't his father be more open-minded like Uncle Edward—always smiling and making jokes?

His mother reappeared in the doorway. "Von, get moving!"

He left immediately for the ballroom. A roomful of guests greeted him, singing: *"For He's a Jolly Old Fellow."*

Unaware of Von's whereabouts, and determined to keep her siblings in line, Ruthia went looking for him. She peeked into his room. Seeing that it was vacant, she turned to leave—that's when she caught sight of the corner of his sketchpad protruding from under the coverlet. As her curiosity got the best of her, she looked down the hall and closed the door behind her. She rushed to the bed and quickly removed the drawing pad.

"What do we have here?" she said, curiously lifting the cover. Her eyes widened, scanning the pages of elaborate sketches of formal gowns, two-piece suits and dresses. "Women's clothing?" She wrinkled her nose.

A knock at the door warned her to conceal the sketches behind her back.

Zanya peeked in. "Von?" She saw her sister standing awkwardly by Von's bed. "Ruthie, what are you doing in here?"

"Close the door. Our brother is in serious trouble!"

Zanya shut the door. "Trouble, how so?"

"Take a gander at this!" Ruthia whipped the pad from behind her back and shoved it at Zanya. "This is Von's!"

Zanya stared at it. "Did *he* show you this?"

"Of course, not! Why would he? It is shameful! Go ahead, open it!"

"I will not! This is Von's personal business,." Zanya defiantly backed away.

Ruthia jerked it open. "Look at it!"

Zanya's apprehensive countenance disappeared and one of pure joy took its place. She stepped closer. "They are magnificent! Von drew these?"

"Don't be absurd. He has no business drawing such frivolity—he's nearly a grown man!"

"Von is extremely talented and there are many famous male designers. Robert Piguet, for example."

Ruthia cut her off, snatching the sketchpad.

"You had better return it to where you found it," Zanya warned.

"Oh no—Mother and Father have a right to know. Von is to be an architect, not dilly dallying with fabric."

"It may just be a hobby."

"A hobby that he had better give up!"

"Ruthia, don't do it. It is his place to tell them." She grasped Ruthia's wrist.

She pulled away. "He may never! He may be planning to abandon his future as an architect with Kade! I won't stand for it!" She stomped out with the evidence pressed against her chest.

Zanya sighed in defeat, rolled her eyes, and followed her. Ruthia's swift exit blew a paper from Von's bureau onto the floor. Zanya retrieved the letter and glanced at the first line.

"Oh...it *is* too late."

Going up against Ruthia would not be easy, but, somehow, she had to protect Von. She loved her father, but he wore blinders when he set his mind on anything. He would be shocked, disappointed, and very angry if he saw Von's sketches—not a pretty picture.

Chapter 2

"Edward's Folly"

"A woman can't drive her husband, but
she can lead him."

—German Proverb

The Sierzik triplets, and their younger sister, Ivy, were in need of nothing material by the standards of the 1930s. Their mother Sophia was a McDonnally—daughter of Hannah, Hiram McDonnally's twin. However, Rahzvon, the head of the Sierzik family, had decided that after his nest egg was lost, that his brood would learn that money was not there for the taking by inheritance—it was to be earned by honest work. Their mother, Sophia, had retaliated, insisting that the children receive a very generous, weekly allowance. After a few objectionable threats, she abided by her husband's wishes and delegated chores necessary to earn the allotted spending money.

This seventeenth birthday party and its bounty shed a new light on the subject of "pin money." After a series of subtle clues, the triplets became well aware of their great-uncle Edward's and great-aunt Naomi's plan to present the celebrated threesome with considerable cash gifts. This information played havoc with Ruthia's well-being. The weeks prior to the party, she could think of nothing else. She changed her mind a dozen times, trying to decide on the perfect use of the cash, whereas, her siblings lost no sleep over the prospect of being well to do. Zanya was a practical, levelheaded girl. She would put the bulk of it into a savings account and the remainder she would spend leisurely on necessities and an occasional token of whim. Von immediately recognized the opportunity for independence. The monetary gift would go toward building his career as a fashion designer by helping fund his room and board in London.

The actual amount of the cash gifts was not divulged. Von and Zanya did not dwell on the unknown; Ruthia was obsessed with it.

On the morning of the birthday celebration, Naomi entered the library. "Darling, I simply have to get a new wardrobe, or at least an up-to-date outfit." She placed a page torn from a catalog over the stamps that he was examining. "Isn't it simply divine? Note the fur trim and the matching gloves. They are all the rage!" she exclaimed.

He stared at the page. "This isn't the cost, is it?"

"Well, yes, dear. It is actually a steal. They charge twice that at Harrods."

He handed her the page and went back to his stamps. "Out of the question."

"Out of the question? Why I haven't had a new outfit in ages!"

"Not now, Naomi. We have enough going out this month for the triplets."

"Fine! If you don't care if your wife looks like a pauper!"

"Now, Naomi—"

"Do not 'now, Naomi' me! And speaking of

the triplets, where are the birthday cards?" she demanded.

"What birthday cards?" He glanced up.

"The ones you picked up from the mercantile last week—the ones I ordered months ago."

"I picked them up?" he squinted in confusion.

"You did, did you not?" her voice threatened.

His jaw dropped as the realization dawned.

"You forgot?" her tone escalated.

"I guess...I did," he admitted sheepishly.

"How could you?" She started to pace, wringing her hands. She stopped and glared at him. "Now, what are we to do? We have less than a quarter hour to arrive fashionably late and we have no cards! And you—you are not even dressed yet!"

He left his chair. "You go ahead without me. I will send Jules over to the mercantile to pick them up."

"The mercantile is closed—locked up for the weekend!"

"Jules can fetch the storekeeper and he can just unlock it!"

"He has left for Sweden to visit Dagmar! *Edward*, I had those cards sent from London. They were specifically designed for the triplets—their names embossed in gold and packets with gold ribbon for the money! How could you?" She stomped her foot.

"I did not intentionally forget them...I remember, now, I went to get them and I met Wiggins the butcher and he was telling me one of those horrid stories and discussing—"

"I do not care if you were discussing plans to prevent another crash of the Stock Market— *I want my cards!*"

"What do you want me to do—break into the shop?" He approached her cautiously. "Be reasonable, Naomi." The look of calculation was growing in her eyes. He grasped desperately for a solution. "I have it! Write a poem and we will put the money in with it!" he suggested enthusiastically.

"*Poem?*" she spat with incredulity. She marched over to the roll-top desk, opened the top drawer, and pulled out three pieces of paper and three envelopes. She shoved them at him.

"Here, Mr. Forgetful! *You* compose something!"

"But dearest, you are the poetry lover—"

"I love poetry. *I do not write it!*"

She spun around and headed up the stairs, muttering comments about the irresponsibility of men.

He was staring at the paper, when he heard her call out, "You have five minutes to prepare those and get dressed!"

He walked slowly to the desk and sat down. He lifted the pen and stared into space.

Roses are red
Violets are blue
I am in deep trouble...
Thanks to you.

"All right, seriously. On this special occasion...what rhymes with occasion? On this special day that we celebrate your birth...Great Scott—what rhymes with birth?" He grimaced then grinned. "Mirth! On this special day that we celebrate your birth, we celebrate it with mirth for what it's worth—forget this! I need a card!" He sat in silence for a second.

"That's it! I *have* cards—lots of them!" He rushed to the oak filing cabinet. "M—M for mementoes." He pulled out a folder bulging with cards. "Aha!"

He quickly spread them out on the table and flipped through them. They were the typical masculine designs, decorated with boats, mountains, horses, etc. He chose a large one with a single tree adorned with white blossoms. He opened it and read the signature.

"Perfect!" It was from a London office. No one would recognize it. "One will suffice."

He went back to the desk, and with a pair of scissors, he carefully dissected the card in half. Smiling broadly, he snatched the pen and turned the front half over.

"Let me think. Tree? Tree!"

Money does not grow on a tree—

but fear not, it's here from Naomi and Me!

He reread it. *Good!* He continued writing:

Best Wishes,

"Hmm?" *Von, Ruthia, and Zanya.* He thought better of his choice and put Ruthia first—she was the only one who would take offense.

Ruthia, Zanya, and Von for a Happy 17th !

With Love,
Aunt Naomi, Uncle Edward,
and Smitty

He pulled out his wallet.
"Uh, oh." He stood helplessly looking at the stack of bills. He tried to cram them into the envelope addressed "Birthday Tidings, Edward."
I need a box. I can connect the card to it.
He glanced down at the envelope, picked up the pen, and modified the original greeting to:

Birthday Tidings, Triplets

from *Edward!* and Naomi

He glanced nervously around the room in search of a suitable box, when Jules appeared in the doorway.

"Excuse me, sir, but Mrs. McDonnally insists that you go upstairs and dress."

"Jules, have you a small box about the size of this card?"

"Sir?"

"A box for these banknotes for the triplets."

"I thought Mum had purchased cards. Did you not pick them up last week?"

"Never mind that! I need a box, Jules!"

"I have a cigar box."

"Fine, please get it and hurry!"

"Aye, sir."

Jules returned with the box and Edward placed the banknotes inside. He carried it to the desk and attached the card with a piece of twine to hold the box closed. He studied the envelope and the unconventional greeting.

"Seventeen-year-olds have no interest in cards, anyway. It will find its way to the dustbin."

The butler watched, listening in wonder.

"Here, Jules. Place this on the hall table by the door, so that Naomi does not forget it."

"Aye sir," he said, narrowing his eyes, knowing that Mrs. McDonnally's memory was not the one in question.

Fortunately, or perhaps not, Naomi and Edward's gift arrived safely at the party at McDonnally Manor.

Ruthia, heading towards the ballroom entrance, carrying the horrid sketchbook, was on a mission to locate her father and notify him of her brother's ill doings. She stopped dead in her tracks at the sight of the tall, redheaded sailor who had suddenly appeared in the doorway. He had his back to her as he conversed with Kade, the adopted son of her great-uncle Hiram and Livia. She swallowed hard—it was Rufus. The older adults would have barely recognized the once skinny, little freckle-faced troublemaker. He had grown as large and brawny as his adoptive father, Tavy. Ruthia tightened her grip on Von's pad, but all thoughts of it drifted away. She then dropped it on the hall side table and floated toward the Titian Adonis. Once within earshot, she paused, and listened, as he and Kade appeared to be catching up.

"How've you been, Rufus?"

"Verra well. I canna believe that I'm back after nigh on to four years."

"Yes, time marches on. Do you know that my sister and brother are already twelve?"

"Amanda and Alex? I remember givin' 'em

rides on me donkey, Pete."

"Yeah, they're quite the pair. They get away with murder. My parents are mellowing in their old age."

"Hiram, mellow? That'll be the day!"

"He had no tolerance when *I* was young." Kade laughed. "Once, when I was about seven, he found me going through his desk in search of some paper. He reprimanded me and banned me from his study for an entire month!"

Ruthia nodded imagining her Uncle's wrath.

"Livia allowed this?" Rufus asked.

"Mother had no choice, but she had comforted me and had said that even she had been on his bad side, occasionally."

Ruthia raised a brow. *Rarely.*

"Yer mother's a saint. I've heard me pa say it a dozen times over."

"She has to be, to have stayed with Father all these years."

"Ye still plannin' to team up with Von and work for Guillaume at the...the architectural firm?"

Kade nodded half-heartedly. He looked to the right. "Ah, there is Uncle Edward. Excuse me, Rufus, I need to speak with the *old* gentleman," he laughed.

"It would appear that he is getting a wee bit scarce on top," Rufus teased.

"Aye, my father's favorite topic—Edward's

baldness. As you can see, Father hasn't lost a strand. I suppose we shouldn't make fun of Uncle Edward. It might not be too long before we will be in his boots!"

"Aye. We should be so lucky to age like Hiram."

"Yes. Too bad, he is not my natural father. I may have had a chance at undying youth," Kade laughed. He gave Rufus a pat on the back. "Welcome home, Rufus. Talk to you later."

Before Kade had a chance to leave, Ruthia cut in from behind them, "Hello, Rufus."

The addressee's confusion was apparent.

Kade verified, "You remember, Ruthia, one of my Cousin Sophia's three lovely daughters."

"Aye...Ruthia, ye hae changed."

"Of course, I have—I am a woman, now," she said coyly. "Might you offer me some refreshment?"

"Do I have a choice?" he grinned.

Kade laughed. "Good luck, my man—you have met your match!" He moved on through the crowd toward Edward.

Ruthia took Rufus's arm and led him to the refreshment table. He poured her a cup.

"Have you been so very lonely at sea?" she asked with concern.

"Nay, Pa and I barely had time to catch our breath. What hae ye been doin'?"

"Me? I graduated. Mother and Father want me to attend college, but I'd rather travel."

"Alone?"

"No, I'd prefer a protective escort—such as yourself," she said, running her hand down his shirt sleeve.

"Ye would, would ye. I'm happy to be on dry land again and I plan on stayin' here for a while."

"I don't plan to leave right away, I—"

"Have ye seen Jeanie Wheaton?" He glanced around the room.

"Yes, but she—"

"There she is! Excuse me, Ruthia."

Ruthia stomped her foot, spilling her punch down her front, as Rufus rushed off to see his childhood sweetheart—another petite beauty. Her brief failure to hold Rufus's attention was a thorn in her side. Ruthia's greatest fear of becoming a lonely spinster was resurfacing. She never claimed to have the beauty to attract a man, but she had hoped that her personality and tasteful wardrobe would capture some young man's heart.

"Fine. You'll see," she muttered, wiping her blouse with a napkin.

Rufus came up behind Jeanie. "Afternoon, me bonnie queen."

The honey-haired young woman turned at his voice. "*Rufus*," she said, astonished.

He grabbed her by the waist, lifted her from the floor, and spun around with her.

"Rufus! Put me down!"

He lowered her down while she smoothed her skirt and primped her hair.

"Must ye be so uncivilized?" she scorned.

"What do ye expect? I havena seen me bonnie queen in almost four years. Yer letters were me only consolation."

"Stop callin' me that—I am not yers," she whispered fiercely, looking around nervously.

"What do ye mean—not mine?" he asked, still smiling.

Marvin Strickland, Naomi's nephew, a head shorter than Rufus and a man of slight stature, came to stand next to Jeanie and addressed Rufus.

"Welcome home, McTavish. We had hoped that you could have attended the wedding," Marvin said, grinning.

"Whose weddin'?" His heart began to pound.

Marvin slid his arm around Jeanie's waist. "Ours, of course. We were married last week."

Rufus felt a knot forming in his stomach and the flush creeping up his face, as his fists tightened.

"Jeanie, ye married this bloke?" he asked bluntly.

"I beg your pardon!" Marvin objected. Jeanie nodded fearfully.

"Find somethin' to do, Strickland. I'd be needin' a moment wit' yer *wife*," Rufus demanded.

"McTavish, I think that you may have had

too much to drink and—"

"Leave, now!" Rufus cut him off.

The room, once bubbling over with conversation and laughter, went silent.

Marvin backed away, warning, "Only a few minutes. I'll be getting a drink, if you need me, darling." He lowered his head and moved through the parting audience. Tavy took Jeanie's hand and led her from the room. Hushed comments followed them out. He escorted her to the end of the hall and stopped.

"Ye couldna wait one more bloody week?" he bellowed.

"Keep quiet. I never agreed to marry ye, Rufus."

"Ye ne'er refused me, either!"

"I couldna be a fisherman's wife. I couldna sit at home worryin', if ye hae been swept o'erboard or worse! I'm not like yer Grandma or Mercy."

"I told ye that me and me pa had plans to start our own fleet!"

"'Tis not the money. I want a home wit' a husband— a husband at *home* wit' me and me bairns. Marvin promised me that. Sorry, Rufus." She pulled her hand from his and darted away.

"Jeanie!" She disappeared into the ballroom. "Our plans, Jeanie," he mumbled.

He stood, staring at the empty corridor, and then turned to the window overlooking the garden. A touch on his arm caused his heart to skip a beat. She had returned. However, he turned to the sympathetic eyes of Ruthia.

She rubbed his arm, "I tried to tell you, but you left so quickly."

"Me bonnie queen," he muttered.

"What did you say?" her voice lilted and eyes danced.

"'Tis not important. I should be goin'."

"What, leave before the party starts? No, sir. A party is exactly what you need. There will be dancing and food and...me!"

He offered her a brief glance.

"Come along, Mr. McTavish. Time and your grandmother's cake heals all wounds."

They walked arm-in-arm back to the ballroom. They were greeted by the partygoers' whispers. Rufus paused by Corrine and Marvel, Jeanie's older sisters. The two were bouncing their babies on their laps while their husbands chatted in a far corner with Edward and Hiram.

"Good evenin', Rufus. We are sorry 'bout Jeanie, but she's—"

"Ye needna explain, Corinne, Wilmoth," he said, nodding, as he pulled Ruthia away. He then stopped. "Sorry, Ruthia, I canna stay."

"Wait, Rufus, there's your father and grandmother. Tavy, Mrs. Dugan!"

Harriet lit up like a Christmas tree, upon seeing her beloved Rufus. "I see ye hae located our fine lad."

"Yes, I did. I just mentioned your cake."

"Well, ye need to be fetchin' a piece for him. I dunna want him runnin' his fist through it, again!" she laughed.

"Aye, ye will ne'er forget it, will ye?" Rufus smiled, hugging his adoptive grandmother.

"Nay, I shan't. Where's yer ma? Yer pa just arrived and is lookin' for her."

Rufus cautiously scanned the room, dreading the sight of Jeanie with Marvin. "I havena seen her."

"I would wager ye hae seen Jeanie *Strickland*," she said, scowling.

Ruthia was discreetly giving her a warning headshake when Tavy grasped Rufus's shoulder and inquired, beaming, "Have ye seen Jeanie, son?"

Ruthia rolled her eyes and shook her head in dismay. "Excuse us, please. Rufus has offered me some refreshment," she announced, pulling him to safety.

When they reached the table, she asked, changing the unsavory subject, "Sailor, how do you like my dress? Mother ordered it from Paris."

"Bonnie," he said, unimpressed. "Is that one o' those new fashions?"

"An exclusive design by—" Ruthia stopped short, remembering her brother's sketchbook. "One moment, stay right here, Rufus. I forgot something." She quickly disappeared.

Chapter 3

"Gift Exchange"

"I looked for that which is not,
nor can be,
And hope deferred made my heart
sick in truth;
But years must pass before a hope of
youth
Is resigned utterly."

—Christina Rossetti

Naomi and Edward's present sat among the many cards and gifts for the triplets. It made quite a showing, placed next to the elaborately wrapped offerings and exquisite envelopes. Naomi feared that she would die of sheer embarrassment, if any of the guests discovered that she and her husband were responsible for the monstrosity. Fortunately, she had taken the opportunity to flip the envelope face down, under the string tied around the faded cigar box. However, if anyone discovered that it was *their* contribution prior to the opening celebration, she was prepared to offer a somewhat valid explanation—placing the burden on her husband and his eccentric sense of humor—anyone who knew Edward, would not have difficulty believing that the cigar box was solely his idea. As for the recipients, the triplets would not be the least bit shocked by his unusual choice.

Meanwhile Ruthia continued with her search for the sketchbook. She checked the hall tables, the buffet next to the veranda entrance, the refreshment tables, and any number of unoccupied chairs.

Nothing.

She moved on to the gift table where she immediately noticed the homely present. She could not wait until the opening to discover the benefactor of the strange package. Who would make such a horrendous offering? She could not imagine. *Mr. Wiggins, the butcher?*

Her curiosity got the best of her. The moment that the coast was clear, she slipped away with it to the hall. Where could she go for privacy? *Of course*, the sanctuary of her great-grandmother Amanda's former bedchamber! She turned the silver key with the green tassel, entered the room, and closed the door. She gingerly removed the envelope and began reading it, as she sat the gift on the dressing table.

"Oh, Uncle Edward—it's you. I'd bet Aunt Naomi threw a fit when she saw what you had come up with," she snickered. Having solved the mystery of the gift-givers, she immediately removed the string and flipped open the box's lid. She peeked in the first of the three envelopes and gasped delightedly, thumbing through the banknotes. After quickly counting them, she frowned with disappointment. *Only three £100 banknotes for each of us?* Now, for the average seventeen-year-old in Scotland, £100 would have been more than an ample amount. But for Ruthia, a mere £300 (an equivalent of $1050) would never suffice; her prospective purchases exceeded that amount by twofold. Of course, there had been no guarantee that Naomi and Edward would give five or six-hundred pounds to each of them, but *only* three-hundred pounds? She returned the envelopes to the box. Her delight had dissolved quickly into confusion and dismay. What could she possibly procure with a mere

£300? Certainly not the new wardrobe; the mink coat alone was at least £170—not to mention, the trip to the Paris fashion show.

She looped the string over the box and paused in deep thought. *Other than Aunt Naomi and Uncle Edward, I am the only other living soul aware of the contents of their gift.* They surely would never refer to the amount; it would not be proper. As far as Zanya and Von were concerned, they would be none the wiser, if the amount for each were significantly less. After all, everyone knew how frugal Naomi and Edward were, never spoiling their children. Besides, they would not be present at the gift opening—a time reserved for the immediate family and hosts.

Ruthia commenced with her plan. She opened two envelopes, removed two one-hundred pound notes from each, and placed it in the third. Now, she had her siblings' £400—a total of £700 for her and £100 each for Von and Zanya. She frowned at the awkwardness that would inevitably occur upon opening the gifts. This would never do—they all had to have equal amounts. She removed the six one-hundred pound notes from her envelope and stared at them pensively. Now they each had £100. *Perfect.* After a moment, she shoved them into the drawer. *A much too obvious hiding place.* She snatched them from the drawer and frantically searched the room trying to calm a growing panic at what she was doing. Her eyes lighted on the pale, quilted satin glovebox, and then the black jewelry box with the ivory inlays. That was it. Once she made her choice, she wiped her now empty hands on her skirt to remove the unwanted perspiration.

"Zanya and Von have no regard for money, anyway," she mumbled, retying the string around the cigar box and replacing the card.

She peeked out the door. All of the guests had vacated the hall and had congregated in the ballroom. She slid through the doorway closest to the gift table and returned the package.

Meanwhile, Naomi was still reeling with embarrassment and contempt for her husband and *his* present. After careful consideration, she attempted to hide the ill-looking package. She casually made her way toward the table and turned. Her eyes widened fearfully.

"Oh mercy!" There it was—the envelope face up, now proudly exhibiting her name next to the name of her incompetent husband. Horrified, she quickly reached for it, just as her oldest daughter, Allison startled her.

"Mother, what is that?" she asked, obviously appalled.

"It's...it's a gift."

"From you and Father?" she frowned.

"Your father's idea of...of a little joke,"

she said weakly.

"But Mother, this is hardly an occasion for such tom-foolery. The society editor from the London paper is here to report on the party!"

Naomi closed her eyes and lowered her head. "Oh, dear."

"How could you let him bring this—this repulsive—this repulsive *thing* into this house?" she asked, looking as though she was going to be ill.

"Allison, it's a long story."

"Long or short, we need to do something or we'll all be laughingstocks."

"I had flipped the envelope to hide our names, but your father must have turned it over."

Allison glared at the package. "A cigar box? Really, Mother! It looks as if you're condoning smoking for the triplets. You can be glad Rahzvon didn't see this. He'd be outraged." She moved close to her mother and whispered, "Remember when he found Von and Kade smoking in the toolshed at the Burns´ Night celebration?" She squeezed her mother's hand. "Don't worry, I'll handle this."

"Take care. There is nine-hundred pounds in there," Naomi warned in a hushed tone.

Allison sauntered over to the adjacent refreshment table and confiscated a white linen napkin. She quickly draped it over the obnoxious present, held it to her chest, and returned.

"What *are* you doing?" Naomi asked.

"I'm removing this eyesore from the public *eye.*"

"But we have to leave it for the triplets."

"Not this. I'll have Miles get a large envelope from Hiram's study and I'll place the cash inside with this ridiculous card."

"All right, but please hurry before your father notices."

"I shan't be a minute."

Naomi watched Allison safely leave the ballroom and then mingled with the guests. Several minutes later, while speaking with the widow Dugan, Naomi noticed that Allison had returned and was talking privately with her husband, Adam. She hoped that Allison had not shared the embarrassing details of the gift with him. Naomi moved stealthily toward the gift table. There, a white envelope, adorned with a blue ribbon was proudly propped against another gift. She cocked her head. *A blue bow? Where on earth had she found it?* Her gaze darted from guest to guest. Then she spotted Addison, her little granddaughter, Allison and Adam's daughter who had arrived at the party wearing a blue ribbon in her hair. It was now missing. Naomi grinned.

Ivy Sierzik ran to the steps leading to the ballroom and then let out a squeal, "Vera!" She could not believe it. Vera's parents had declined the birthday invitation, just a week earlier.

"Ivy!" Vera called.

"You came. What happened?" They exchanged hugs.

"Father finished his blueprints early and said that we shouldn't miss a family party."

"Where are your brothers?"

"Graham couldn't come. He had a scheduled jumping event. He's staying with a friend. But Royston is here," she said, glancing toward the ballroom. "*Somewhere.*"

In the meantime, Rufus was perusing the crowd. Jeanie was nowhere to be found—neither was her new husband, but *there* was a familiar face—familiar, but different—a much younger version. He approached her slowly.

"Excuse me—but hae we met?"

"Yes, some time ago. However, we've both been elsewhere—you out fishing and I was away at school."

"Yer the spittin' image of her," he chuckled.

"I've heard it a thousand times. I do wish that I, like Ruthia, had my 'own' countenance." She offered her hand to him. "Welcome home, Rufus. Zanya Sierzik, Sophia and Rahzvon's daughter."

"Aye and ye hae grown up, too."

"Well, a little. No 'short' jokes, please."

"I saw yer sister, Ruthia."

"Yes, she grew a little taller."

"Quite a bit taller," he teased.

"Perhaps, I enjoy being close to the ground. It gives one a sense of security," she only half-smiled.

"Ye even smile like Sophia."

"Well, I can assure you that although I favor my mother, I share my father's personality. Father says Ruthie is another 'Phia.'"

Rufus looked passed Zanya, as a lump formed in his throat; Jeanie and Marvin were laughing a few yards away.

"Miss Sierzik, could we be continuin' this conversation on the veranda?"

"It would be my pleasure, *Mr.* McTavish."

The two left the ballroom under the suspicious and protective scrutiny of Hiram McDonnally, Zanya's imposing great uncle. Rufus may be the honorable Henry McTavish's son, but this did not discount the fact that he *is* a sailor.

"So, Zanya, do ye enjoy bein' tiny?"

She sighed and walked over to the railing above the fountain.

"No, I don't. I was born first and the biggest of the three of us. That was the last time I was the largest. Ivy is even taller than me."

"'Tis not so bad." He ruffled her hair like he would a little girl's.

To his surprise, she turned scowling. "Do you have any idea how impossible it is to find a decent wardrobe when you fit in little girl's clothing?"

He laughed, "Nay, nay, I don't. So you're jealous of Ruthia?"

She turned back toward the evening sky. "Maybe."

"Ye dunna get along wit' her?"

"Ruthie and I are typical sisters—sharing and sparring, whereas Von...he and I have a mutual respect for one another's opinions and interests."

"And Ivy?"

She laughed. "We share our special moments. She's forever bombarding me with hilarious questions and her crazy philosophy, but she gives me endless ideas for my writing. What about your family?"

He looked down at the fountain's arcing geysers and leaned on the railing. "Me family is different than most. We're more like dory mates floatin' across the sea, weatherin' the storms. Probably because me ma and pa, Tavy and Mercy, became me best friends before they became me parents; 'tis funny sayin' their names, now." He hesitated and then continued, "Phemie and I were thrown together when Ma nearly died havin' her. She's me champion and kindred spirit. "He turned to Zanya. "Aye, after fishin' side-by-side wit' Pa for the last few years, the older I got to be, the more we seemed to be like brothers, instead of pa and son, not that I have any less respect for him."

"And Mercy?"

"She is different than me first ma who was a woman of few words. I can talk to Mercy; I feel close to her. She understands me, maybe 'cause she lost her parents...I'd be so lucky to find a wife like her."

Zanya glanced over at him and then smiled.

Ruthia returned to the frantic search for Von's sketchpad. The proof that he had deviated from a proper future as a prominent architect had vanished, now missing from the table where she had left it. She had retraced her steps several times, but it was nowhere to be found. After a final inquiry with the housekeeper, Twyla, Ruthia gave up the search and went to find the jilted sailor. He had disappeared, as well. His absence did not please her. Before she could begin her search for him, her mother requested everyone's attention.

Sophia began, "I want to thank all of you— I mean *Rahzie* and I want to thank all of you for attending the seventeenth birthday celebration for our beautiful babies. In a moment, the music shall commence and from the appearance of the refreshment table, I will be ordering more food from the kitchen!" she laughed. "Feel free to put any notes of congratulations on the table. Thank you. Oh, and will our triplets please come up here? Von, Ruthia, Zanya!"

Ruthia and Von immediately found their way to their parents. Zanya did not.

"Zanya, Zanya!" Sophia called.

After Hiram stepped out on the veranda and retrieved her, Zanya rushed to join her siblings. Rufus sauntered into the room after Hiram. Ruthia's jaw dropped.

With a fierce whisper, she attacked her sister, "*What* were you doing with *my* date?"

Zanya ignored her inquiry.

Sophia began again, "You all know how triply blessed I feel, having raised these fine children and Ivy, of course—our little surprise, but I shall let their father speak on this auspicion occasion."

Auspicious, Phia, Rahzvon muttered mentally. He nervously looked over the audience and cleared his throat.

"What does a father of four healthy, somewhat level-headed children say after all these quickly passing years?" He regarded the listeners for a second. "Phia and I never expected to be raising three infants at the same time, but thanks to family and friends, we survived—twister and all."

The audience laughed.

He continued, "The good Lord must have thought that we did a decent job or he wouldn't have given our little Ivy to us."

A sea of smiles met him.

"In all sincerity, my life couldn't be more perfect. I have a lovely, talented wife, and four children who have made me very proud to be their father."

Ruthia immediately glanced at her brother. How proud would their father be of his only son, if he knew the truth about Von's plans?

Rahzvon ended his speech with a word of gratitude. "I want to thank you for sharing in the celebration of this very special day. Thank you...I may also take the liberty to add this special announcement—"

"Not another Sierzik, Gypsy!" Tavy called out. His wife, Mercy nudged a disapproving elbow into his ribs.

The crowd roared.

Rahzvon cleared his throat. "No, no! Our family is complete. However, one of the Sierziks," he said, placing a hand on Von's shoulder, "well, this coming fall, my namesake will proudly take the position at the London architectural firm of Zigmann McDonnally."

The following applause brought a rose flush to Von's face.

With that ending comment, Ruthia grasped Zanya's wrist and whispered, "I seriously doubt it and you had better leave Rufus alone! You knew that I was planning to spend the evening with him!"

"I knew no such thing. Rufus can decide for himself. He can spend time with anyone he chooses," she retorted.

The two rivals spun around to seek the object of their affection and then shared a look of disappointment. He *had* chosen. Young Smitty, Naomi and Edward's sixteen-year-old daughter of extraordinary beauty, was now laughing and smiling up at "their" sailor.

Zanya shrugged and left her steaming sister to find Martha Wheaton, a close friend who shared her interest in writing.

"Hello, Martha," Zanya greeted her with a smile.

"'Twas a bonnie speech yer pa gave. I wonder what me pa would say 'bout six daughters and one son," she giggled. "So will ye still be attendin' college in the fall?"

"Probably. Will you write to me?"

"Aye, if I *find* the time," she said, grinning.

"Is Conrad Strickland monopolizing your every waking hour, Martha?" she teased.

She bit her lip and looked shyly to her feet. "Well, if ye promise to keep a secret—"

"I do—I do!" She latched on to Martha's arm.

"Well," she laughed at her friend's enthusiasm, "it may not be too long before *I* am saying—'I do.'"

"How exciting, Martha! When?" She grasped both of Martha's hands.

"He hasn't asked yet, but soon I believe. He'd better not wait too long or I shall be an ol' maid of twenty before Christmas!"

"You're not that old and now women are waiting much longer to marry."

"Perhaps. What 'bout ye—any prospects?"

"None." She shrugged. "I'm not looking, either."

"What 'bout Kade?"

"No, heavens no, Kade's a cousin of sorts."

"He's not. Yer not kin at all—Kade is adopted. He is really *not* a McDonnally."

"I know, but—"

Martha spotted him on the opposite side of the room. "There he is. He's quite easy on the eyes. Think o' it, Zanya—you could end up wit' the McDonnally name. Ye would be a McDonnally like yer ma was."

"That's silly. Besides, she was never a McDonnally, really. Grandma just gave Mama her maiden name to protect her."

"Did she ever discover who her pa was— yer grandfather?"

"No, I don't think that my grandmother wants Mama to know."

"'Tis not fair to ye or yer ma." She shook her head.

"It may be for the best."

Martha looked past Zanya. "Look. What are those lads up to?"

Martha's younger fifteen-year-old brother Bruce, Guillaume's eleven-year-old son,

Royston, and Adam and Allison's nine-year-old son, Adam Jr. were huddled in a corner of the ballroom.

"Give me the pen!" Royston demanded.

Zanya watched him snatch something from Bruce. Then she caught a glimpse of what that something was. It was Von's sketchpad!

"Oh, no!" Zanya darted towards them, when Marvin Strickland intercepted.

"Lads, what are you doing?" he asked, jerking the sketchpad from them. "Whose is this?"

Zanya started to raise her hand, but took a step back and declined. How could she reveal Von's secret to Marvin? The boys scattered. A second later, Marvin and the sketchpad were gone, lost in the crowd.

Martha stepped next to her. "Zanya, what was it?"

"I'll tell you later. I have to find Ruthia."

Chapter 4

"Kindred Spirits"

"Take my share of a fickle heart.
Mine of a paltry love:
Take it or leave it as you will,
I wash my hands thereof "

—Christina Rossetti

In her search for her sister Ruthia, Zanya consulted her sister, Ivy, first. "Have you seen Ruthia?"

Ivy stepped away from Vera and Beryl, Jake and Agnes Kilvert's daughter, to reply.

"Yes. She was helping clean up Marvel's baby. It was an awful mess. He had grabbed Marvel's cup of punch. They are over there." She pointed to the north side of the room.

Zanya made her way over to them and noted the stain on Ruthia's dress. "I guess you were in the line of fire, as well."

"Yes, well..." she nervously smoothed her skirt, not about to reveal that the stain was a result of her earlier disappointment in Rufus's desertion.

"Ruthia, I need to speak with you. It's urgent."

"Excuse me, Marvel." Ruthia turned back to Zanya. "What is it?"

"Von's sketchpad."

Ruthia's eyes widened. "What about it? Have you seen it?"

"Yes, I have and several others have, as well," Zanya scorned.

"Where is it?"

"Marvin has it. He took it from young Bruce, Royston and Adam Jr. They have defaced it from what I can tell! What are you going to tell Von?"

"I am not telling him anything and either are you. We are equally guilty of being in his room and looking at those horrid designs."

"I wasn't the one who took it—you were."

"Zanya, you had better keep quiet about this. It's for the best. Now, Father and Mother will never know about Von's silly drawings. Now, I need to speak with Conrad," she said curtly.

"Conrad? Why? Are you having him ask Marvin for the sketchpad?"

"Heavens, no, I want to dance with him."

Zanya frowned. *Martha's Conrad?*

Martha Wheaton was a friend so dear that she actually seemed to be more of a sister than Ruthia or Ivy, not that Zanya would ever confess it. *Ruthia was cutting in on Martha's interest in Conrad? I have about had it with Ruthia's fickleness. She is always looking for greener pastures.* She shook her head and headed for the refreshment table.

The party continued with much gaiety and laughter. Everyone seemed to be enjoying him or herself. Even Rufus curbed his jealousy and anger over the Jeanie-Marvin union. Ruthia suffered no remorse for her unscrupulous pilfering and Zanya, although peeved by her sister's theft of the drawing pad, was relieved that Ruthia would not be making an embarrassing scene over the sketches. Naomi was now at ease knowing she and Edward's gift would not be a social disgrace. She was dancing with Hiram, her childhood sweetheart, now nephew by marriage.

She looked up at him with saddened eyes, "I cannot believe that the triplets are nearly full grown adults. Time has gone so quickly."

"Aye, it seems only yesterday that *we* were young and without a clue as to where life would lead us."

"After all that happened with my father, I never imagined that I would end up as a part of the McDonnally clan."

"Nomi, you were destined to be a McDonnally—one way or another." He smiled down at her.

Edward cut in, "Dearest, I need to speak with you."

Hiram nodded and bowed out gracefully.

"Don't be alarmed, Naomi, I am sure that there is a logical explanation, but... someone has made off with our gift for the triplets."

"Sh! No one has stolen it. It has taken on a new look—a more presentable one."

"New look?"

She glanced to the gift table. "Do you see that large white envelope with the blue bow?"

He nodded.

"That is our gift—minus the cigar box," she whispered.

"But why did you—"

"Never mind, what is done is done. Now we can hold our heads up proudly, without shame."

"Was it so awful?"

She narrowed her eyes and frowned slightly. "Absolutely, Edward."

"Yes, dearest."

The music began again. He placed his hand on her waist and took her hand, as they then moved gracefully across the floor.

Edward scanned the crowd and inquired, "Dearest, where's Smitty? I haven't seen her for quite some time."

"I don't know." Naomi perused the sea of the partygoers.

They paused beside their eldest, Allison. "Have you seen your sister?" Edward asked.

"Not since I saw her with Rufus after Rahzvon's speech."

"Rufus? Smitty's with Rufus?" Naomi swallowed hard.

"They were out on the veranda when—"

"I'll be back." Edward was off like a shot. He entered the veranda, where he found Marvin showing Jeanie a book of some sort.

No Smitty or Rufus.

Edward returned to Naomi. He shook his head. A concerned expression fell across her face. Rufus had not done anything to warrant fear in the worried parents...not recently. His slate was clean—so to speak. He was no longer the little scallywag that broke windows and punched cakes. Just the same, his previous behavior still left a haunting doubt as to his true character. Doing their best to remain calm and fair in their judgment, Edward and

Naomi moved from couple to couple, casually asking if anyone had seen their youngest daughter.

Finally, with Naomi's insistence, Edward left to inquire about *Rufus's* whereabouts; he too, was missing. Edward slowly approached Tavy.

"Henry, how was your stay at sea?"

"Fine, Edward. It gave Rufus and me a chance to work side-by-side, like pa and son."

"Ah yes...we certainly miss *your* father. Lochmoor Glen is not the same without Joseph. He was a fine man."

"Aye, he was as close to me as me own pa. Ma has been doin' her best to get along, alone, but Rufus and I came back to help her wit' the move."

"Move? Where to?"

"Eloise has asked Ma to live wit' her in Town—both bein' widows and best friends."

"*London?* Harriet *and* Eloise? I can't imagine it." On seeing his wife approaching, Edward quickly excused himself to speak with her.

Naomi rushed to him. Her questions came out in rapid succession.

"Where is he and where is my young, innocent daughter? What did Henry say?"

"Dear, Harriet and Eloise are relocating to London," he said solemnly.

"London? *No.* When?"

"Very soon, I suspect. Tavy and Rufus

returned to help Harriet with the move."

"My goodness...both of them leaving Lochmoor Glen," she mumbled.

"It stands to reason—Eloise's family *is* living there, now."

"It will be so different without them," Naomi lamented.

"The adjustment of losing both Joseph and Albert was difficult enough," Edward agreed.

"Yes, especially at family gatherings such as this. There is such a void. It must be awful for both of them."

"Yes, unbearable. I still cannot believe that they are gone..." Edward sighed.

"Gone!" She grasped his wrists in a panic.

"Smitty!" His glance darted around the room.

"Where is Rufus? What did Tavy say?" Naomi demanded.

His jaw dropped. "I forgot to ask!"

"Sometimes I think that your amnesia never left!" she scoffed. "*I'll* ask Henry." She moved quickly towards him.

"Henry! Have you seen Rufus?" she asked with urgency.

Tavy's smile disappeared. "Nay, what's he done?"

"Smitty was last seen with Rufus. Neither is present."

Tavy's face grew more serious. Rufus was twenty-three, Smitty seven years younger.

Tavy's negative response to the news further distressed the already nervous parents. Tavy appeared to force a smile and replied encouragingly, "Not to worry, I'll find him...them."

Tavy made a beeline for the stairs to the second floor, checking, en route, any room with a door ajar, despite his true concern for the closed ones. Keeping a hopeful attitude regarding his son's integrity, he made a quick check of the parlor and dining room. After first bypassing Hiram's private study, his second thoughts gave him cause to return and search it.

Empty.

He paused in the main hall. "This house is too blasted big!"

He sprinted towards the kitchen upon hearing youthful laughter. He paused at the entry and listened. The immediate silence led him through the doorway. He swallowed hard at the sight before him. He had finally found them—not innocently chatting, but engaged in a passionate kiss.

"Rufus!"

Rufus quickly removed his hands from Smitty's waist and stared at his equally surprised father. It was not *Smitty* with Rufus, but Dara Wheaton.

After a breath of relief and a bit of embarrassment, as Dara was close to Rufus's age, Tavy apologized and asked to speak with his son. Dara could not conceal her embarrassment, as well, and darted from the room.

"What are ye doin' lad?"

"I'm *not* a lad n'more—I'm a man," Rufus objected.

"The party is *upstairs*," his father cautioned.

"Not for me."

"Dunna be insolent!"

"Pa, did ye not see her? She couldna wait one bloody week! She purposely married that bloke Marvin before I got back! How dare she?" he shouted. "I loved her wit' all me heart and soul! And she loves me!" he yelled, as his eyes welled up.

"Son, I dunna believe that she truly loved ye, or she wouldna hae married—"

"She doesna love him! She wanted his money and security!"

Tavy considered this side of Jeanie. Of course, she wanted financial security; she grew up in a home with five siblings and barely enough to eat. Tavy had been a good, loving father to Rufus, in every sense, but this one time, he was unprepared to help his son accept the finality of the relationship with Jeanie. Although Tavy was not a stranger to heartache, having temporarily lost Mercy to Guillaume, he knew the situation was different. He and Mercy were together, whereas Jeanie was married and no longer available.

How could he advise Rufus? *His* dream had come true—he and Mercy were happily married and they had not only raised Rufus together, but had had a child eight years ago— their precious daughter Phemie.

His angelic daughter's sweet voice interrupted Tavy's thoughts. Phemie had magically appeared to help her brother, as she had done so many times before. She and Rufus had shared a special relationship, since the day she was born; they were destined to be close companions for the rest of their lives. She ran to her distraught brother and hugged his leg, as she was quite petite for her age. Her diminutive size was a source of many jokes directed at Tavy and his parentage, for he was a large brawny sailor and her mother Mercy was definitely of *hearty* stock. All of the good fun teasing alluding to Phemie's similarities to the tiny jeweler, Mr. McDenby, was not appreciated by the irritated sailor.

"Please, don't be sad, Carrot-Top," Phemie pleaded with tear-filled eyes. "I love you."

Rufus picked her up and hugged her. Watching the touching scene, Tavy thought back to her arrival in Rufus's life.

Mercy had become very ill in the last month of her pregnancy with Phemia. Dr. Lambert had feared that an infection was spreading to the unborn child and had instructed that Mercy remain bedridden for the term of the pregnancy.

"Pa, we're not goin' to lose Ma?" Rufus had whispered outside her room.

"Nay, we can't—we love her too much to allow it. The good Lord wouldna do that to us."

"Aye, Pa."

The next hours were crucial.

Tavy looked at the alarm clock on the nightstand. The healthy, tiny Phemia had arrived shortly after midnight, but Mercy's condition was critical. Her weakened state left the care of the newborn to her father and fifteen-year-old brother.

"Pa, we need Grandma Dugan."

"Aye, but she needed to visit wit' her sister. Not to worry—we need only follow Dr. Lambert's orders."

"I wish he didna leave us." Their isolated home in the refurbished lighthouse seemed all too far from the closest village.

"A doctor's on call all o' the time. He needs to be goin' where he is needed."

"He's needed here for Ma!"

"We hae our instructions, Rufus. Now, do ye think ye can care for the bairn?"

"Aye," Rufus had replied hesitantly.

"While the bairn's milk is warmin', check for any word o' ill weather on the shortwave. A storm's brewin'."

"Will we hae to go inland?"

"I'd hope not. Yer ma shouldna be moved," he said gravely.

The caregivers slept only a few of the next

forty-eight hours. Fortunately, the storm was a mild one. Tavy closely monitored his wife. Rufus, fed, diapered, rocked, and comforted his little sister. Tavy had watched his son quite naturally take on the role as a surrogate parent; the infant was quite content in her brother's arms. Mercy's days of recovery brought joy and relief to the two men. Equally, the bond between Phemie and Rufus completed the family unity.

From that first day, Rufus and Phemia had a connection unlike most siblings. They were always aware of the other's well-being, despite the difference in their ages. Shortly after Phemia's second birthday, Rufus rolled the tractor. Screaming for him, she flew from the house, as fast as her little legs would carry her. She had not witnessed the accident, but had still sensed it. When Rufus chose to join his father with the fishing crew, Phemia deemed their separation as unacceptable. She expressed her disapproval in the many hours she spent drawing pictures and later writing letters to the two cherished men in her life, begging for their quick return. Their occasional visits did not suffice.

Now, Rufus was back and hurting. Phemia tried desperately to console her broken-hearted Carrot-Top. In a few short minutes, she had Rufus laughing at her imitation of Minnie Mouse. With very little effort, she convinced him to return to the party as her escort.

Tavy had now forgotten all about the missing Smitty McDonnally. After learning that she was not in the company of Rufus, her parents were somewhat relieved. Fortunately, for them, shortly thereafter, Smitty appeared in the ballroom, laughing with Ivy and Vera. Where she had been was a mystery to all, except to her, Ivy, and the *one* with whom she had kept company.

Smitty was Edward and Naomi's first child together, as Naomi had adopted Allison as a small girl prior to her marriage to Edward. Smitty had grown up as nearly an only child, as her sister Allison was married and a mother by the time Smitty was three. Smitty spent many hours in her parents' company. Naomi raised her without the aid of a governess and Edward's position in the McDonnally business kept him home, busy in the library. Smitty, like Allison, spent many hours sharing time with her father while studying his prized stamp collection. Although Smitty's relationships with her parents were close ones that she cherished above all else, she often felt the pressure of the generation gap. She seldom confided in them about what she considered "serious" matters. Ivy, who had always seemed to be a surrogate little sister to her, was her primary confidante. Smitty never really developed a close friendship with either Ruthia or Zanya, but their younger sister Ivy, too, enjoyed having a special friend in her cousin living so close by. She lavished in the attention of the older girl and she and Smitty spent much of their free time conspiring secretly alone. Today was no exception.

In the third floor corridor, Ivy asked Smitty with apparent dismay, "Are you certain that you want to go through with this?"

"Oh yes!" She looked down at her solemn little friend. "When you're older, Ivy, you'll understand. Don't worry, nothing will change *our* friendship. We will always be there for one another."

Ivy gave a little smile and nodded.

Chapter 5

"Moment of Truth"

"The world is too much with us,
late and soon,
Getting and spending,
we waste our powers;
Little we see in nature that is ours..."

—William Wordsworth

After the guests had left, the triplets gathered with their parents, Hiram, and Livia for the official opening of the gifts. Edward and Naomi had no intention of remaining—until, that is, Ivy pleaded for them to stay so that Smitty could visit with her. Ivy was at the mercy of the green-eyed monster; she had no interest in her siblings' gifts and desperately wanted a distraction during the annoying event. It would be years before she would be the beneficiary of such generous offerings.

This unexpected turn of events sent Ruthia into a tizzy. Edward and Naomi *would* be present for the gift opening. Riddled with guilt about removing the money, Ruthia sat uneasily with Zanya and Von while the bounty was delivered from the third floor.

"*Ruthia,*" Sophia warned, "stop fidgeting. It's so unbecoming. The gifts will be here, soon enough."

"Sorry, Mama."

"Excited about the surprises you're about to receive?" Edward teased.

Ruthia nodded nervously. He had no idea. The fact that no one knew that *she* was the one who had removed the £600 did little to relieve her tension. She needed to calm down, so as not to appear suspect.

It took quite some time for Twyla to return—two trips in fact. Miles, the butler, was otherwise engaged in assisting Eloise with the tea and scones. Eloise had insisted on serving as the McDonnally cook for the evening, as one last contribution before her retirement.

Ivy and Smitty sat giggling and whispering on the window seat.

"I think Groucho with his grease paint mustache is funnier than Harpo," Smitty said.

"Fine, but you know who's by far the most handsome actor," Ivy grinned.

"Ronald Colman!" they yelled in unison.

At that moment, Naomi decided that their exuberance needed to be retired to the kitchen for afters; she sent them on their way, chatting about Joan Crawford's dancing abilities, Jimmy Durante's nose, and his talent as a pianist.

Ruthia wished that she could follow them out. Her nervous stomach now seemed to govern her every move. There they were, not four feet away—the gifts, but where was Naomi and Edward's? The cigar box was not among the other presents. How could this be? It was a miracle!

As the triplets opened the presents, the generosity and thoughtfulness of the guests became quite apparent. Although many of the locals did not share such a position of wealth as the McDonnally clan, the time and care in choosing gifts for the triplets was remarkable.

The widow, Harriet Dugan, Hiram's former tenant and Tavy's adoptive mother, had donated three of her late husband Joseph's hand-carved twiglets to each seventeen-year-old. Any outsider to Lochmoor Glen would not understand the significance of this gesture. However, the village residents knew it to be a keen token of love. Joseph had carved dozens of these realistic, small, wooden creatures. For years, they were displayed in Harriet's parlor with various backdrops. A shingle reading "The Twiglets" hung proudly above their front doorstep. These were dearly beloved contributions. Harriet first conceived the idea when Wilmoth Wheaton turned seventeen, twelve years ago. Having little income for gifts, with Joseph gone, Harriet chose to distribute the Twiglets throughout the homes of Lochmoor Glen, to spread the spirit of his memory. Her choice for each recipient was proof that she was in tune to the interests of the younger generation.

The Sierzik children, like all of the Lochmoor Glen young ones, were enchanted by the incredible detail and variety of the Twiglets. The triplets opened the boxes from Mrs. Dugan, secretly knowing what would be inside—but exactly which ones would they each receive? That would be the surprise.

Zanya opened hers first, revealing a frog, a rabbit, and a bird in a library setting.

"Look at all the little books! I'll visit Harriet tomorrow and thank her. I'll display them wherever I live." She turned happily to her sister. "Open yours, Ruthie!"

Still unnerved by the missing cigar box,

Ruthia smiled and began removing the paper wrapped from her gift.

"How positively precious," Sophia remarked, admiring the duck, cat, and sheep donning bonnets adorned with tiny flowers and ribbons. They were posed in the little millinery.

"It is perfect for you, Ruthia," Livia commented.

"It is," Ruthia repeated, trying to justify anyone being charitable to her, considering the crime she had committed. She stared at the beautiful gift.

"Your turn, Von," Rahzvon noted. "I can bet what this backdrop will be."

"How much?" Hiram chimed in.

"Hiram!" Livia objected.

"Ignore them, Von. Go ahead open yours," Sophia insisted.

Von glanced around at the observing guests and slowly removed the paper from his box. Odds were—the backdrop would reveal a building or bridge. However, Mrs. Dugan had remembered. Von smiled with delight. The little dory manned by the sailor dog was floating on the sea. A shark and whale hovered beneath the bow. Von, as a small child, had always asked Joseph to show him the "ship," knowing that each time Joseph presented it, would offer a tale of his seafaring days.

"Guess the cards, have been played." Edward laughed.

"What do you mean, Uncle Edward?" Von asked.

"You have to abandon your plans of becoming an architect!"

All eyes were on Edward. Von to abandon his plans to be an architect?

"Of course," Edward continued. "Yes, to become a sailor! Joseph's Twiglet's have spoken."

Ruthia raised a brow and turned to Zanya. "Abandon his plans, indeed," she whispered.

Zanya took a breath, and made no reply. She immediately insisted that they open the small envelopes from Hiram and Livia and then passed them out.

"I'll open mine first," Ruthia said, tearing open the envelope. She curiously removed the gold embossed card and scanned it.

"What does it say?" Zanya asked, anxiously.

She looked up at Hiram and Livia. "Oh, my, I...I don't know what to say."

"Read it to us," Von cut in.

Ruthia held the card up. "This entitles the bearer of this certificate: one week at the Ritz Hotel at Place Vendôme, Paris, and admittance to the fashion show (with a suitable travelling companion)." She let out a scream of delight, "I can't believe it! Thank you!" She ran to hug the benefactor's.

Zanya beamed at her sister's joy. *Everyone knew*—how much Ruthia longed to travel to

Paris and desired to hob nob with the aristocrats at the exclusive fashion show. She may be a Sierzik by birth, but the world was aware that she *was* a McDonnally—Hannah's granddaughter and Hiram's great niece.

On the other hand, Von obviously found it difficult to withhold his pangs of jealousy. His expression grew grave. This fashion show was the most highly acclaimed in the world. That is where *he* belonged.

Zanya glanced at her brother and quickly volunteered to open her envelope to divert the attention from her brother's gloomy demeanor. She immediately removed the card, read it, and burst into tears.

"What is it?" Ruthia asked with concern.

Hiram put his arm around Livia whose eyes had welled up, as well.

Zanya's trembling hand presented the card to her mother.

Sophia glanced nervously at the second, gold trimmed card and read aloud. "To the bearer of this card, Livia and I offer our two horses—Hunter and Baron with the services of our groom for their care."

Zanya looked up to Hiram. "But why?"

He smiled. "Because Zanya, you have always loved our horses and have always wanted one of your own. Hunter being a retired, older lad, I dare not burden him with my weight, anymore."

Rahzvon immediately looked away

uncomfortably. His daughter had always wanted a horse—it was true, but he had said that it was impossible—it would be too expensive for the horse's care. Now, Hiram had fulfilled Zanya's dream in one swift move. Ruthia recognized the familiar spark of jealousy between the men; Zanya was so happy, that she did not notice. Although Zanya preferred to exist in her own world, sitting in a comfy chair, equipped with pen, paper, and a hot cup of tea, she did have a special place in her heart for animals. As a child, she had adored the family cow, and of course, horses, too. Ruthia noted that Zanya often preferred their company to that of people. Zanya had explained that horses were genuine in their feelings and much less complicated than fickle humans. Ruthia felt her sister *thought too much* about everything.

Livia added, "As for Baron, he is Hunter's closest companion, since we lost Duff. The doctor advised me to give up riding, since my back trouble after carrying the twins. So, Zanya, you have two mounts...if you want them."

Zanya wiped away her tears of joy, "Yes, yes!" She flew at her great aunt and uncle and could not hug them enough.

Ruthia was happy for her sister, but saw no need for her having *both horses*. After all, she too, loved horses. However, she quickly realized that although Zanya now owned the two wonderful animals, she could not ride two horses at once; Zanya was not a trick rider. Yes, there would always be a horse available for *her* to enjoy rides across the moors with her sister, the only hobby that she shared with Zanya.

The time had come for Von to reveal the contents of his envelope. All knew it had to be architecturally related. It was.

However, after cautiously reading the card, Von expressed his sincere gratitude, "Thank you, thank you!"

Ruthia snatched it from him. She read, "Certificate for a line of credit at the art supply store in London."

Hiram grinned, "You will need a variety of drawing tools and pencils in your line of work."

"Yes, I will," Von said, smiling from ear-to-ear.

Ruthia narrowed her eyes. Rahzvon, nodded at Hiram with approval after a commanding nudge from Sophia. Zanya proudly patted the forearm of their now content brother.

"Alas it is time for ours!" Edward said, glowing.

Ruthia held her breath, as Naomi took the large envelope tied with the blue ribbon from the teacart that held the remaining gifts. But what was this? It was not their gift. It was not the worn cigar box attached to Edward's card. *Edward's card?* Had she read it wrong? That was impossible. Her head was spinning to sort out the details while she scanned the teacart for the cigar box. She glared at the "new" package, offered.

Zanya handed it to Von. "You open it Von," she suggested, encouragingly.

Von took it quite willingly and removed the bow. He struggled to unseal it, as it was not cooperating. Ruthia sat back speechless and observed—totally out of character for Ruthia, the usual center of attention.

Von reached into the envelope and pulled out the card, displaying its envelope. He held it up for Ruthia and Zanya to see.

"Very nice," Ruthia said weakly.

"Quite original," Zanya giggled.

Naomi shook her head and glared at her creative husband.

Von slid the card from the envelope, showed his sisters the tree adorning the front, and read aloud the greeting. All were laughing except Ruthia who could barely breathe at this point and the very embarrassed Naomi.

Von then removed one envelope and distributed the other two to his sisters. Each looked inside. Ruthia swallowed hard, knowing that she had to muster up some enthusiasm.

"My goodness, Aunt Naomi, Uncle Edward, cash!" Zanya said gleefully.

"Aye, young adults like nothing better than a fistful of banknotes!" he laughed.

"*Edward,*" Naomi reprimanded him. "Use

it wisely, children."

"We will," Zanya reassured them.

At that moment, Ivy appeared to check out the booty. "How much did you get, Von?" she asked, wide-eyed.

"It's not polite to ask," Rahzvon abruptly reminded her.

"Sorry, Von." She bit her bottom lip and glanced away in embarrassment.

Edward straightened in his chair. "It's quite all right, Ivy. Go ahead, Von, count it," Edward added proudly. "If you have enough time," he joked.

"Very well, I will." He pulled the banknote from the envelope. "One-hundred pounds!"

Edward's proud countenance vanished in a split second. He said nothing. Ruthia watched, knowing that he was baffled, wondering where the other two-hundred were. Naomi exchanged a look of concern with him.

Ruthia jumped at the opportunity before they might comment and quickly removed hers. "One-hundred!" she said ecstatically.

Zanya followed suit, "One-hundred. Thank you, both!"

Hiram, confused by the small amount, knowing Edward and Naomi could have afforded much more, forced a smile. The stock market dive had required some tightening of the purse strings, but Edward surely could have afforded, at the very least, double the amount of the gifts.

Edward glanced away from Hiram's questioning eyes. Now portrayed as a Scrooge, Edward was equally confused and upset. He had given three-hundred pounds to each, but did not know where it had gone.

This drama was too intense for Ruthia. "Well," she announced and stood up, "Thank you All of you! We need to get things cleared away. Come along, Zanya, Von!"

The triplets, loaded down with gifts, were gone in a flash, but the cloud of suspicion hung heavy over the parlor. Edward's confused wife shared his silent contemplation of the remarkable modification of their gift. She and Edward had agreed on three-hundred pounds for each. The baffled couple avoided contact with the proud parents, as well as Hiram and Livia.

Edward left his seat and helped Naomi to her feet. "We had better call it a night. It has been quite a day," Edward said, straightening his coat.

Naomi lifted her pocketbook from the side table. "Yes, it has been delightful. Thank you for having us."

"You sound like strangers!" Hiram laughed. "Are you not still members of the clan?" he teased.

"Of course," Naomi smiled.

It is a wonder, after the showing of that pittance of a gift, Edward thought.

"Ivy, where's Smitty?" Naomi asked.

"Uh...probably still in the kitchen. Wait here. I'll get her."

Naomi and Edward had made their way to the front door of McDonnally Manor when Smitty appeared.

The three then drove off to Brachney Hall. While her parents remained quiet, Smitty chatted a blue streak with her take on the celebration. Her parents did not comment until suddenly, her father shouted, "You stay away from that sailor! Do you hear me?"

Smitty sat back, stunned. She wanted to explain that Rufus was not, nor ever had been, the source for her affection—but dare she make them suspect that there might be someone else?

Their peculiar silence was now becoming unbearable. Her mother kept looking periodically from her father to the window, while he remained unusually stern and focused on his driving.

When they arrived home, her father excused himself and retired to the library. "I'll come to bed in a while," he muttered to her mother, as he entered the hall. He said nothing to her.

"Certainly, dear. Up to bed, Smitty," her mother said mechanically.

"Yes, Mama." She turned to her. She was staring blankly down the hall.

"Mama?"

"Yes?"

"Is everything all right?"

Naomi stared briefly at her. "Go on to bed; it's late."

No kiss, no "good night?" Her mother seemed to be in a trance. Nothing was right. There was a problem between her parents and she was suspicious that *she* was the problem. Her sister Allison had told her that their parents were frantic in their search for her, after Allison reported seeing her with Rufus. Smitty started up the staircase.

Chapter 6

"Suspicions"

"Who loves well is ready to forgive."

—Ukrainian proverb

Edward took a seat in the overstuffed chair by the library window. The moonlight shone across the room before him. He revisited the events of the day regarding the triplet's gift:

First, he had placed the bills in the three envelopes and then into the cigar box.

Then what?

Jules placed the cigar box in the hall for Naomi to take to the party. He remembered making a comment about Naomi and her forgetfulness.

Jules? No, surely Jules had not done something with the money.

"Jules," Edward called.

Surprisingly, the butler quickly stepped in from the hall. "Yes, sir?"

Edward was far from prepared to accuse his friend of many years of pilfering the six-hundred pounds from the gift box, but he had no choice but to inquire.

"Jules?"

"Yes, sir? Are you in need of something?"

"Nay...about the cigar box—"

"Sir, I must apologize."

Edward sprang from the chair. "For what?" he asked fearfully.

"After you handed me the gift, Miss Smitty bounded in. Do you remember?"

"Yes."

"I gave the box to her to deliver to Mrs. McDonnally, instead of leaving it on the hall table. I had promised to help the cook pack some afters for the party, and was short of time."

"*Smitty?*" Edward mumbled. *Smitty, a thief?*

"Not to worry, sir. I saw Mrs. McDonnally with it, shortly thereafter. It was presented to the Sierzik children, was it not?"

"Uh...yes, yes, it was. That is all, Jules, good night."

"Yes, sir."

Edward returned to the chair. Smitty? Impossible—the girl was in want of nothing. But if not her, then who had taken the money? Jules had been ruled out...which left who exactly?

"Wait a minute!" *The gifts were re-wrapped—taken out of the box and put in the white envelope with the blue bow. Who had switched it?*

Edward's eyes nearly popped from his head. "*Naomi?*" he exhaled on a breath.

Edward pondered the unthinkable—could Naomi be responsible for the missing cash? *Why?* Did she think it was too much? No, she had thought three-hundred pounds was barely suitable, considering their income. He squirmed at the implications that there could be an unknown dark side to his life-long partner. He grimaced at the unacceptable explanation that Naomi wanted it for herself. No, not sweet, innocent Naomi. But...she had shown him pictures of the fur-trimmed suit with the matching gloves, countless times and he had complained that the outfit was unscrupulously overpriced. Then there was that heated argument.

Unfortunately, it all made perfect sense: his wife had a motive and the opportunity. She had switched the money from the cigar box to the envelope. But no harm was really done; the triplets, nor anyone else, was wise to the missing banknotes. However, Hiram and Livia surely considered Naomi and him to be penny-pinchers.

His thoughts went back to Naomi. *She was distraught when she heard Von announce the amount.* Could she have been pretending? Well, she probably never suspected the amounts to be broadcasted at the party— especially in his presence and they were *not* supposed to be present for the gift opening.

He slapped his thighs and stood up. Now what? Dare he confront her? No, he need not. Her shocked face and silence on the trip home were proof of her guilt. She knew where the money had gone and she knew that *he* knew.

"I will retire, now, and wait for her confession," he said, leaving the library. He paused in the doorway. "After, I have another piece of carrot cake and milk. The Lord knows that I need it."

In the master bedroom, Naomi sat in front

of the mirror brushing her hair. *Why would Edward give them only one third the amount of what we had decided?* He would not have. He had been adamant—three-hundred pounds, not a penny less. He would not have changed his mind. He had acquired a cigar box to hold all of them. Besides, he was obviously flabbergasted when the amounts were announced...So then where had it gone? Only Edward had handled the money—wait, no, he had not been the only one. *Allison. She had exchanged the wrappings.*

She dropped her brush to the table. Could it be—her grown daughter, mother of her grandchildren—stealing? It was not possible. She would never steal from anyone, especially not from the children of her dearest friend, Sophia.

Naomi rubbed her forehead—but Allison was so insistent upon making the gift presentable. Naomi held her stomach, feeling suddenly ill. What other explanation could there be? And for Heaven's sake, why?

Naomi walked slowly to the bed, sat down, and leaned back. Suddenly, it came to her. Allison and Adam needed a new stove. Adam refused to allow his wife to dip into her trust fund. They would not purchase the stove until he could pay for it and that would take months. Allison had confided in her that she was resolved to the fact of not having a cook in her employ, but could not bear to use the old stove any longer; she had her eye on a new AGA stove. Naomi had advised her daughter to wait patiently for her husband's sake. Allison had originally agreed, could she have changed her mind? Naomi closed her eyes, tormented by her suspicions.

Edward arrived a few minutes later, wiping a bit of icing from the corner of his mouth. She lay quiet and motionless. He dressed for bed and slid in beside her.

"Edward, we have a problem."

"We have, dear?" he replied innocently.

"Dearest, it is about the gift for the triplets."

"I know."

She sat up. "You know what happened to the money?" she asked in surprise.

"Don't you?"

"Yes, but how did *you* discover it?"

"Is it not fairly obvious? Only one person made contact with the gift before it was presented," he explained.

"Yes," she agreed, but was confused. She had never mentioned that Allison had rewrapped it.

"And you were that one person, my dear," he said compassionately.

"Me!" She flew from beneath the covers. "You believe that *I* took the other six-hundred pounds? How dare you Edward Caleb McDonnally? How *dare* you accuse me of breaking a commandment?"

His attempt to be understanding had backfired. She was not confessing—she was blatantly denying the act. He left the bed.

"Calm down, Naomi. I am not accusing you. I understand that you wanted that fur dress thing with the matching—"

"You think that I stole money from our beloved nieces and nephew for the self-serving purpose of purchasing—" Her raging expression took him aback.

He went to comfort her and she shoved him away.

"Stay away from me, you...you traitor!"

"But dear, you removed the money from the box—what was I to think?" he pleaded.

"For your information, you distrustful, disloyal man—I did not put the cash in the envelope!"

"I know that you didn't—you needed it and you took it—that is not stealing."

"I didn't take the money, nor did I rewrap that atrocious excuse for a gift that you created! Allison did!"

He took a step back in horror.

"Allison," he mumbled. "Our Allison?" He was dumbfounded. He could not imagine Allison doing such a despicable deed and even worse, he had falsely accused the love of his life. He approached Naomi slowly.

"We need to get to the bottom of this."

The suspicions did not stop there. The

next day, Sophia and Allison were having tea when the subject of the party came up.

"You did a glorious job with the party décor, Sophia," Allison remarked and sipped her tea.

"Thank you. I think that I will miss the hours preparing for it—exhausting that it was. I spent nearly three months!"

"I suppose the triplets were thrilled with their gifts," Allison said, smiling.

"Yes, everyone was incredibly generous. It took Twyla several trips to bring the presents down from the ballroom."

"Did Harriet give the usual Twiglets?"

"Yes, millinery shop for Ruthia, the nautical scene for Von, and the library for Zanya."

"Were they surprised at Mother and Father's gift?"

"They were...and frankly, I was a little myself. Allison, I didn't know that they were suffering financial difficulties."

"What do you mean?"

"One-hundred pounds is nothing to scoff at...I just thought..."

"One-hundred!" Allison nearly spilled her tea.

"That is still quite a bit of money for one's so young."

"Sophia, you must be mistaken!"

"No, that was the amount."

Thoroughly confused, Allison's thoughts

went back to the moment she had rewrapped the gift. Her Mother had warned her to take care with it—the three-hundred pounds in each envelope. Could her mother have been mistaken? Something was wrong—very wrong. Where had the money gone, if it *was* there? She had to find out. She had to confer with her mother.

Allison grabbed her pocketbook from the table and started for the door. "I'm sorry, Sophia, but I have a lot to do today. I'm having Corinne Wheaton do my hair. May Addison continue her visit with Ivy?"

"Certainly."

"Please, tell her that I'll come for her later this afternoon. Thank you for the tea."

"I'll tell her," Sophia agreed and looked suspiciously after her hastily departing friend.

Allison walked briskly out the main door. *One-hundred?* Where did the other six hundred go? She stopped in her tracks. "That's it! Someone took it from the gift table and removed the extra money and then returned it." *But who?* It had to have been done discreetly.

She drove to Brachney Hall, considering the possible suspects. The only one alone with the gifts was...Twyla, the new housekeeper. Sophia had mentioned that Twyla had taken several trips *alone* with the gifts from the ballroom. "How dare she take employment and then steal from the party!" *I must tell Mother!*

When she arrived at Brachney Hall, she continued with her mission and ran to the door.

"Mother, Mother! Where are you?"

Edward met her in the front hall. "Allison, what's wrong?"

"It's about the gifts," she said anxiously.

"What gifts?" he asked, pretending to have no knowledge of the matter.

"The ones from you and Mother for the triplets!"

"What about them?" he asked hesitantly.

"This may come as a shock to you, but the triplets each received only one-hundred pounds of it!"

"I know."

"Who told you?"

"I was there. It is alright, dear."

"No it's not. You had given them three times that amount," she added, shocked by his response.

"I understand," he said with a sympathetic tone. "I've given it a lot of thought and I'm not angry."

"Not angry about six-hundred pounds stolen right beneath your nose? Why not?" she asked in disbelief.

"Dear, your mother and I know how difficult it is for you, cooking on that old stove for a family of four and—"

"Old stove?" She put her hands on her hips. "What are you talking about, Father?"

"You needed the money for an AGA stove and—"

"You're not suggesting that *I stole the money?*" she shrieked.

"Dear, I'm not angry. Your mother told me how you switched the gifts to the envelope and—"

"Mother accused me of stealing from my best friend's children who also happen to be my distant cousins? Agh! I cannot believe this! You blame me, your daughter, before you place the blame on a woman who is practically a total stranger and who entered the McDonnally mansion under false pretenses *and* a hidden agenda?" she screeched.

"Who did what?"

"Twyla, that new housekeeper, stole the money! Not me!"

She stomped her foot and ran out, slamming the door behind her.

Once again, Edward stood awkwardly with one foot planted firmly in his mouth. Naomi came rushing down the steps.

"Was that Allison's voice that I heard?"

He nodded forlornly.

"You *didn't?*"

"I did. She stormed out."

"Oh, Edward, I didn't want her to feel bad about it. She wanted that stove, so much."

"She doesn't feel bad about it, trust me."

"She doesn't?"

He closed his eyes and shook his head. "She's as mad as a bear with its paw stuck in a beehive."

"I don't understand. Allison felt no remorse for taking the money?" she asked, confused.

"No, dear, because she didn't take it. Your daughter is not a thief, but thinks I'm a cad, thanks to you!" He glared at her.

"Thanks to me?" her eyes narrowed.

"You charged her unjustly. It was Twyla, Hiram's new employee, who took it. Stands to reason, she brought the gifts down from the third floor."

"Twyla? We got along famously. I can't believe it." She folded her arms in a huff and sighed.

"Naomi, I can't believe that you convinced me that our daughter was the thief!"

"Edward, I did no such thing!"

They went silent.

Naomi finally spoke, "I guess I did...but you accused *me*."

He let out a sigh. "I accused nearly everyone, including Jules. You need to straighten things out with our daughter. I need to apprise Hiram of the treachery in his household." He took Naomi by the shoulders. "Goodbye, Naomi. Good luck," he said with his head lowered at the prospect of what he had to do.

She grasped his wrists and looked into his

eyes. "Goodbye, Edward. I wish you the same," she said sadly, considering what had started out as a blessed event.

Neither of them had noticed the arrival of their young daughter at the top of the stairs to witness the very *final* sounding exchange.

Smitty stood on the landing above the parlor in shock. What had she done? She was responsible for a major falling-out of her parents. Her mother must have had supported her feelings for Rufus, while her father had adamantly objected—she would always be "Daddy's little girl" in his eyes. Now they were splitting up. A tear trickled down Smitty's face. "I've destroyed my family," she whispered fearfully, "and I don't even have feelings for Rufus." Overwhelmed by the entire situation, she walked slowly to her room. How could this be happening?

With mixed feelings, Edward entered his nephew Hiram's home. He wanted to warn Hiram before Twyla walked off with the family silver, but did not relish the prospect of witnessing Hiram's reaction when he learned of her stealing from his beloved triplets.

While waiting to be announced, Edward peeked into the parlor where Ivy and Addison chatted on the window seat.

"Hello, Grandfather," Addison called.

He offered a brief wave before Miles directed him into Hiram's study. The girls watched him enter. A moment later, a loud crash drew them closer to the door.

Hiram bellowed, "She *what?* My employee stole six-hundred pounds from my great nieces and nephew—their *birthday money?*"

Ivy and Addison shared a wide-eyed look.

Hiram shouted, "That woman will never work another day in her life as anyone's house servant or anything else! I shall have her incarcerated!"

"Now Hiram, this may be her first offense."

"It may not be, either."

"I know I am hardly the one to say this, but you should give her a chance to explain."

"Explain, after stealing from *children?*" Hiram's brows furrowed.

Edward rubbed his chin in deep thought. "What if she was desperate—has a dying relative in need of medical attention or something?"

"'Something' is right! A bad case of sticky fingers!"

After hearing the sordid details, Ivy and Addison ran to locate the three victims of the crime.

Chapter 7

"Black Sheep"

"Never ruin an apology with an excuse."

—Benjamin Franklin

The two excited girls found Von, Ruthia and Zanya in the Sierzik parlor in the East Wing.

Out of breath, Ivy gulped and announced, "Twyla—Twyla is getting sacked!"

"It's true," Addison confirmed. "I heard it all."

Von left the rocker. "Why is she being asked to leave?"

"Because she's a thief! This is serious!" Ivy exclaimed.

"A thief?" Ruthia said casually, slowly approaching her younger sister.

"Yes. Twyla stole from you and you and you," she claimed, pointing at each of her siblings.

Von took Ivy by the shoulders. "Stole what, Ivy?" he demanded, curious if Twyla was responsible for his missing sketchbook.

Addison explained, "She stole £600 from your birthday money from Grandma and Grandpa McDonnally."

Zanya turned to Von. "Two-hundred from each of us?"

"Uncle Hiram is having her incarcerated," Ivy added.

Ruthia backed away from the others.

Zanya and Von examined her now pale face. Why was she silent, without an opinion? Normally, she would have thrown a fit about the missing additional birthday money.

Von took hold of her arm. "Ruthia, what

do you know about this?"

"I...I'm speechless," she mumbled.

Zanya studied Ruthia's face, and then dismissed the two messengers, warning them, "Say nothing about this to anyone."

The two nodded and ran off.

Von and Zanya backed Ruthia into the couch and gently pushed her to sit.

"Confess, Ruthia. What do you know about this?" Von demanded.

Ruthia rolled her eyes. "You're making a mountain out of a mole hill. It is really nothing."

"Nothing?" Von scowled. "A woman's life is at stake—she may go to *prison!*"

"That's impossible! They have no proof that she stole it!"

"How do you know that, Ruthia?" Zanya asked, glaring.

"Ruthia, tell me that *you* did not steal from Zanya and me," Von commanded.

The guilty party did not make eye contact with her jury.

Zanya could barely speak. "How *could* you...Ruthie?"

"Don't look at me like that! I was only borrowing it, temporarily. How was I to know that Uncle Hiram and Livia were paying for my trip to Paris!"

"Ruthia! I am disgusted," Von scolded and left the room with the disheartened Zanya trailing behind.

Ruthia shouted after them, "Don't tell them! Please! I will give it back!"

Her pleas fell on deaf ears. The betrayed siblings reported directly to their parents, who fortunately cleared up the situation with Hiram and Edward before the innocent Twyla fell prey to Hiram's rantings.

At Brachney Hall, Edward returned before Naomi, where he found Smitty sobbing on the couch in the drawing room.

"Darling, why are you crying?"

"Oh, Papa, I am so sorry. I never meant to cause trouble between you and Mama."

"Trouble, you?"

The flustered girl could not get out the words quickly enough. "I know that you don't approve of Rufus. I promise I will never speak to him again! Face it! You and Mama will probably never accept my dating anyone, but I *am* a grown woman. Times *are* changing. It is different than it was when Allison was growing up, but this is no reason for you and Mama to split up. Please, convince her to come back to us!" she pleaded. "We are a family."

"Dear, dear Smitty, there is nothing wrong between your mother and I."

"But I heard you saying goodbye and good luck to each other," she sniffled.

"That? My dear lassie, your mother and I had some serious family matters to tend to and we were wishing each other luck. That is all."

She hugged him as tight as possible. "I'm so glad—I could not live without the two of you!"

"Nor could we, without you, Love."

Forced to confess her sins, Rahzvon first ordered his black sheep-of-a-daughter to go to Brachney Hall to make a not-so-formal apology to all those involved in the debacle of the missing cash.

Secondly he demanded, "Ruthia, go and get your brother and sister's money. We will discuss your punishment when you return," he said sternly.

She went directly to Amanda's room where she opened the vanity drawer. She lifted the folded hankies. It was gone! She yanked the drawer out, sat it on her lap, and rummaged through it.

"It's not here!" *Wait.* That is not where she had hid it. She quickly replaced the drawer, shoved it closed, and opened the jewelry box.

Not there!

"Good grief, where is it!" she panicked. "I need to calm down...I was going to put it in the drawer, but I decided to..."

She grabbed the satin glovebox and grinned with victory. She opened the lid. Her eyes widened.

It was not there.
Stolen!

She began checking every drawer in the dressing table. Nothing. She scurried over to the chest of drawers. She noted the un-fashionable lace shawls, and knitted sweaters and then felt around beneath them. Nothing. *The nightstand!* She looked in the wafer-thin drawer and the two shelves below it. Again, nothing. She plopped down on the bed and closed her eyes. *Think, think, think. Where else could it be in here?* She scanned the room. Then felt under the mattress. The money was nowhere to be seen or unseen. It had to have been moved, but by whom? *Twyla.* She had cleaned this room. She must have taken it.

Ruthia started to pace about the room. But now, what was she to do? How could she return empty-handed? No one would believe her, especially if she suggested that Twyla was responsible, again, even if she was.

Her life was over. She slowly returned to the parlor where her father waited. In one hand he held the *Scottish Motor Traction Magazine* that he had been reading; the other he extended, palm up toward her.

"Hand it over," he said gently.

"I can't. I don't have it. It's missing from the place that I hid it."

"*Ruthia.*"

"Honest, Father, I searched everywhere. It's gone! I hid it in Great-Grandmother Amanda's room. Someone took it. It had to be Twyla—she cleans that room."

"Ruthia, you're in no position to make accusations of thievery."

"But Father—"

"Ruthia, I'm finished discussing this. You have one week to come up with the money. In the meantime, you may split your one-hundred pounds, giving fifty to your sister and fifty to your brother. Needless to say, your mother and I are *very* disappointed." He threw down his magazine and left his daughter speechless.

The unsuspecting housekeeper lay on her bed in the maid's room reading *The Good Earth*. The stocky woman, who barely fit into her uniform, laid down the book and sat up when Ruthia stormed in.

"Where is it Twyla?"

"Where is what, Miss?" she asked while smoothing the sides of her silver hair that was neatly pulled back in a bun.

"The money in Great-Grandma Amanda's room!"

"My dear, I have not a clue as to what you are referring."

"Don't *dear* me! The money—the six-hundred pounds that was in the glovebox!"

Twyla stood up and loomed over her accuser. "Now, Miss, you had better watch your tongue. Has no one taught you to respect your elders? And how dare you accuse me? I shan't take this abuse! I shall report this to

Master McDonnally."

"You won't have to! I will!" Ruthia backed away from the irate woman and disappeared through the kitchen to the hall.

Twyla leaned back and continued reading until her gaze left the print and moved to the light fixture above her. Yes, she had discovered the cash and yes, she had taken it. There was a distinct possibility that the young, Sierzik lass may report her suspicions to Master McDonnally. This could be the beginning of the end of her housekeeping career at the McDonnallys' or worse. She let out a sigh. She definitely needed the employment and this roof over her head, rather than that of a prison. Her employer was generous in his pay, gave her a clean room, uniform, all that she could eat, and most importantly respect. Risking all of this was hardly worth a mere six-hundred pounds. She sat up, reached beneath the mattress, removed the pilfered cash, and stuffed it into her apron pocket.

Minutes later, she was on the third floor, stealthily closing Amanda McDonnally's bedroom door behind her. The money was safely out of her possession—for now. It lay hidden beneath the handkerchiefs in the vanity drawer. Fortunately, her employer made no mention of Ruthia's accusations.

The week passed and her siblings barely acknowledged Ruthia's existence. She did not take the shunning mildly. She made a vow to get even with her estranged brother and sister; no one was going to treat her like a common criminal. Yes, she had made an error in judgment and no, her siblings would have never committed such a heinous mistake. Although she was not perfect—like the promising author, Zanya—her sister had no right to punish her. She was not her mother. And Von—he may not be a thief, but he *was* a liar, deceiving his parents about his plans for the future. How dare he act so high and mighty and ignore her? Ruthia gave no regard to the fact that she had already upset them enough by dishonoring the seventeen-year bond be-tween them. She was out for revenge and Von, in her opinion, was an easy target.

She addressed her likeness in her vanity mirror, "Fine, dear brother, pretend that I am invisible, but I have enough ammunition to blow you out of the water! I know your secret—your plans to scribble your life away in fashion! And Zanya, sweet Zanya, I am not sure how to deal with you, but take care. One opportunity arrives and I am taking it!"

Ruthia did not wait long before she made her move. The setting was perfect: Eloise Zigmann's farewell supper with the family. Everyone would be there: her parents, Zanya, Von, Great Uncle Hiram and Livia, Kade, Trina and Guillaume, and Great Uncle Edward and

Naomi. Eloise's best friend—the village gossip—Harriet Dugan would also attend.

Adam Jr. and Addison were ready to entertain the remaining five children (Hiram and Livia's twins, Alexander and Amanda; Guillaume and Trina's children, Royston and Vera; and Ivy, at their home. Addison had just completed decorating her extravagant dollhouse with her mother. Adam Jr. had received an electric train for his ninth birthday from his McDonnally grandparents, Naomi and Edward, and he was working on displaying it properly.

Allison preferred to stay at home with the children for the evening. Although she dearly loved Eloise, her former future mother-in-law, sharing the table with her ex-fiancé Guillaume and his wife, her once, dear friend Trina, would be nothing less than awkward. She harbored no feelings of remorse or bitterness over the dissolution of the relationship with Guillaume, but the three of them had gone their separate ways. However, the amiable relationship between their offspring remained intact. As Adam was away on business, Allison invited Smitty to keep her company that evening. She accepted, albeit reluctantly.

The farewell celebration was to begin promptly at seven o'clock. Twyla prepared the meal, but the retiring Eloise insisted that she make the after—one last carrot cake for Edward. The grand dining room table had all its leaves in place, covered with the beautiful, white lace cloth. The flowers were imported, as MaryAnn Wheaton had, unfortunately, lost her greenhouse to a hailstorm. Ruthia struggled with second thoughts about disrupting dear Eloise's farewell party, but her anger drove her to continue with her plan.

Once the guests were seated, Hiram stood before his chair, smiling.

"It is wonderful to see all of you here, tonight. Eloise, my sister Hannah sends her best regards from Paris for your retirement and assured me that she would be paying you a visit in Town in the very near future."

The guest of honor nodded and returned the smile.

"It is not every day that a man has the opportunity to employ a woman as talented, trustworthy and tolerant as you, Eloise."

Ruthia glared at Twyla, as she placed the appetizers in the middle of the table.

Hiram continued, "There are only a few hundred words that describe you, Eloise. You are an excellent housekeeper, tremendous cook, and for many years, my caregiver. You survived my mood swings that occurred, more often than not."

"I'll say," Rahzvon cut in, with a grin.

Snickering filled the air.

"Aye, aye," Hiram waved away the laughter.

"But I am improving...correct Livy?"

Livia shrugged and rolled her eyes, which she knew would stir another roar of laughter. It did.

"Granted, not many women would have stayed in my employ, as you did, Eloise. Your dedication to this clan, and dear Albert's unsurpassable work ethic—bless his soul—were unmatched by any on this earth. The love that you, Albert and my brother Guillaume brought to this old mausoleum truly made it a home."

He reached for his goblet. With tear-filled eyes, he raised it.

"With eternal gratitude, I wish you happiness in your new home, Eloise Zigmann. We all love you and will dearly miss your daily presence."

Chapter 8

"The American"

"Better to remain silent and be thought a
fool than to speak out and remove all doubt."

—Abraham Lincoln

Many tears fell that evening of the farewell party before the first course was served. It was not until the fourth that all melancholy had vanished and laughter filled the dining room. Ruthia watched and waited for that perfect moment.

Guillaume was commenting on the construction of the Oakland Bay Bridge in San Francisco and remarking that his new associates, Von and Kade, would accompany him to check out the new Lambreth Bridge in London.

Ruthia's moment had finally arrived.

Hiram off-handedly addressed Von and his son, "Von, Kade, we will soon be celebrating your farewell dinner."

Kade offered no reaction and Von only half-smiled.

Guillaume spoke up, "I am proud to report that my lovely, industrious wife, Trina, not only prepared the little cottage for Mother, but she has spent hours cleaning out the large store-room in my office. She had shelves and a larger window installed, and acquired two, rather grand, antique drawing tables." He smiled at Kade, then Von.

Hiram chimed in, "Trina, you should have waited for Kade and Von. They could have helped you. Right, lads?"

Ruthia glared at Von. He slowly turned to her.

"Perhaps not," Ruthia said casually, laying

down her fork, as she witnessed her brother's anxious expression evolving.

Rahzvon immediately responded, "*Ruthia.*"

"Just stating the facts, Father."

This set Sophia off. "Young lady, your brother and cousin Kade are hard workers and grateful to Trina. You, apologize immediately for that remark."

"*Ruthia,*" Rahzvon warned.

Ruthia noted Zanya's trembling hands grasp Von's. She was successfully paying Zanya back, as well.

"I was only remarking that *Von* can't help with the architectural firm, if he's not there, Father."

"Of course he is going to be there!"

"I highly doubt it," Ruthia stated pointedly.

Sophia turned to her son. "Von, what is this all about?"

The color had left Von's face. Kade sat back, disengaged from the conversation.

Ruthia remained silent and smug while Zanya squirmed as their brother's panic began. Then, to everyone's surprise, Zanya jumped from her chair.

"I will tell you what she means—but I will tell you with the pride of a loving sister, not a ruthless one! Unbeknownst to the rest of you, my dear brother Von, is an extremely talented artist!"

Rahzvon interrupted, "Zanya, we're all

aware of his talents. That's why we have been supportive of his new career."

"Not his architectural talent—his extraordinary talent as a—"

Ruthia cut in, "As a dabbler in dresses!"

"A what?" Rahzvon and Hiram shouted in unison.

Von slid down in his chair.

Zanya resumed her soapbox speech, "He only needs minor mentoring to become one of Europe's finest!"

"Finest what, Von?" Rahzvon demanded. Von dropped his head.

Zanya looked to her brother, then demanded, "Raise your head proudly, Vonmanstrong Sierzik!" She turned to her shocked audience. "My brother will someday be famous in the world of women's fashion design—as famous as, Elsa Schiaparelli, Madeline Vionnet, or Coco Chanel! He need only to accept the position under the expert instruction of a famous designer in London. As the Chinese say, 'Pearls don't lie on the seashore. If you want one, you must dive for it! And that is what Von must do!"

This powerful tribute left the diners speechless, with the exception of Harriet Dugan who muttered, "Fashion design?"

Livia, immediately restrained Hiram by a grasp on his arm. Ruthia sat with baited breath, waiting for their parents' responses. They sat bewildered. Ruthia was pleased, until she noted Kade smiling at Zanya, apparently approving of her *display.*

Then, the unthinkable occurred. The women, save Harriet, exchanged broad smiles, rose to their feet, and applauded. Ruthia wrinkled her nose and shook her head in defeat. Her plan *may* have failed.

After another day of Ruthia's pouting had passed, Zanya knocked on her bedroom door.

"Come in."

Ruthia sat at the dressing table.

"Ruthia, after your beastly betrayal, Von suspects that you have the sketchbook, but does not care to speak with you. There has been enough discourse in this family of late. You have caused enough havoc. You need to go to Marvin Wheaton and ask him for it."

Ruthia turned around to face her. "Marvin? Why would he have it?"

"Because I saw him take it from some of the younger boys at our party."

"*You* saw them, I didn't. *You* should be the one to approach Marvin." She returned to shaping her thin brows with the tweezers.

"No, Ruthia! Enough is enough! Take responsibility for your mistakes. Now, you go retrieve it or I'm telling Father that you stole it from Von's room! Do you really want to completely destroy the relationship with your only brother and further anger, Father?"

Ruthia stared at her reflection and then,

looked up to her irate sister's face. Yes, she had caused enough damage to the family unity. She laid the tweezers onto the dressing table and applied a puff of powder to each cheek.

"Very well, I'll go."

"Good. Now, shake a leg!" Zanya left, closing the door behind her. Ruthia walked over to her wardrobe.

"Hmm...what to wear. Conrad is still visiting." She smiled and picked a smart, two-piece suit, and prepared for the unpleasantness to follow.

Twenty minutes later, Ruthia walked up the path to the Strickland charming ivy-covered, stone residence. The sight made her heart hurt and her fingertips tingle.

"Someday, I shall have a beautiful home," she vowed. Apparently growing up in the tiny, off-kilter family home and now residing in the colossal mansion had left more of a mark on her than she had realized.

Taking a deep breath, she rapped the doorknocker.

The butler answered, "Good afternoon, Miss."

"Hello, I am Ruthia Sierzik. I wish to speak with Marvin, please."

"Come in. Master Strickland shall return within the half hour. Do you care to wait?"

"Yes, thank you."

She had barely taken her seat in the

massive drawing room before Conrad arrived.

"Ruthia!"

"Conrad." She offered him her hand.

"So you couldn't avoid my charm any longer."

"Correct as usual. It's been an absolute bore without you," she giggled, but stopped short. Her jaw dropped. There *he* stood—a stranger, tall and blonde with perfect curls—a golden version of her Uncle Hiram. He moved from behind Conrad.

Conrad turned to him. "Ah, yes—ignore this oaf," he laughed.

Ruthia stepped closer, in awe of the uncommonly handsome guest.

"Mr. Seton," Conrad touched her hand, "this is the bonnie Miss Sierzik. Ruthia, Mr. Stanford Seton."

She quite willingly offered her right hand.

"My pleasure, bonnie Miss Ruthia Sierzik—an unusual name, 'Ruthia'."

"A combination of Sophia and Ruth—my mother's names," she mumbled, staring at her hand in his.

"Stan's determined to honor us with his presence for the next few months," Conrad chuckled.

"Yes, I'd hoped to attend Marvin's wedding, but business delayed me."

"That's a shame. It was a beautiful ceremony, wasn't it Conrad?" Ruthia remarked, studying the stranger's response to the subject of matrimony.

"I guess, if you enjoy that kind of thing."

"Have you known Marvin for some time?" she asked.

"Four years at the University of Edinburgh Business School. We were apartment mates—sorry, I believe you refer to them as 'flats.'"

"You're an American like Aunt Livia," she said, pleased.

"Indeed, I am and proud of it. I found Marvin's *new* flat mate to be quite a prize."

"Jeanie *is* quite pleasant—and about my age."

Conrad laughed, "Right, Ruthia," he said dubiously.

Stanford grinned, "Now, Ruthia, I'd guess that you are a few years younger."

"Not really, I assure you. I look young for my age."

Conrad rolled his eyes. "It's a shame Stanford missed your birthday party last week—your *seventeenth.*"

"Oh, hush, Conrad," she shot back at him, annoyed at his making fun of her.

"Dare to join us in the garden, young miss?" Conrad teased.

"I suppose." She looked to the ground until Stanford offered her his arm.

"Mr. Seton, I always wanted to visit America," she said, taking his arm. "Please tell me all about it."

He escorted her to the wrought-iron bench

and sat beside her.

"What would you like to know?"

"Excuse me," Conrad interrupted, "but I have a date with my new sister-in-law's sister."

"Martha?" Ruthia asked.

"Who else? I hope that you don't mind entertaining this bloke for a while until Marvin returns."

As all designs on Conrad had vanished; she focused on Stanford's shy, dimpled, boyish smile and replied, cow-eyed, "Not at all."

"Very well, I'll see you two later."

Ruthia offered a brief wave, and then insisted, "Go on. Please tell me about America."

"The cities are different." He folded his hands in his lap. "A lot of chain stores have sprung up in the last few years."

"That *is* different. We sell chains in the jewelry stores."

Stanford slapped his thighs and burst out laughing, "Ruthia, you're priceless."

"What's so amusing?" she asked, indignantly.

"Nothing. You misunderstood, that's all. *Chain stores* are a group of stores, built and stocked the same, throughout the country. Like links in a chain."

"Oh." The flush of embarrassment came over her. Oh, how she despised looking foolish.

"There's Woolworth and S.S. Kresge, which are variety stores similar to your village mercantile. The J.C. Penney stores are middle-class versions of your Harrods department store. Western Auto stores specialize in car parts and the Piggly Wigglys are food stores."

"Piggly Wiggly?" she snickered. "You silly Americans. What else?"

He spread his arms, describing, "The cities are overrun with automobiles. Over thirty-six million have been made. And just about everything you pick up is made in Japan. The Japanese are undercutting prices and booming in many industries."

"I see. So, what do Americans do in their spare time, besides shopping?"

"Water skiing, baseball, and going to the movies. Dance marathons are also popular. I enjoy canoeing or spending Saturdays at the beach. Kool-Aid and corndogs—that's the American way."

Cool-Aid? Corn dogs? She dare not ask for fear of further embarrassment.

She studied his face. She felt that meeting this man was too good to be true. She had never met anyone like him and fearing that their time together was short-lived, she had to inquire. "I don't mean to interrupt, but are you going back to America when you leave here?" she asked, looking down at her hands, now folded in her lap.

He placed a finger under her chin and lifted it. "Why do you ask? Does it matter?"

She could not breathe. He had touched

her face. "I...I was just wondering if I might see you, again."

"I might be persuaded to extend my visit, given enough *incentive*."

She could not be more pleased. She considered his name. *Stanford Seton?* "Seton's a Scottish name," she said, trying to withhold her smile. He was Scottish, too. How perfect.

"Yes, it is. I have Scottish ancestry. That's why I chose to attend school in Scotland. I was actually born in a borough outside New York City."

"So, you enjoy seeing the world?"

"Yes, very much so—I've even visited Peru."

"Peru—how exciting!" she blurted out. She quickly covered her overzealous reaction with a casual, dignified inquiry, "Why Peru, Mr. Seton?"

"It's always fascinated me—home of the Incas. Why I even attended the Inca Festival of Inti Raimi, near Cuzco."

"What's that?"

"June 24th, the Festival of the Sun." He cocked his head proudly. "I will have you know that I have a handsome, handwoven poncho that I purchased there. I also visited the Archbishop's Palace in Lima. It was rebuilt a few years earlier in '24."

"How does it fair in comparison to our castles?"

"Oh, the façade is *extremely* ornate."

"Do the Perui... uh, do they speak English?"

"The *Peruvians* speak Spanish." He leaned back. "Ah, yes, it's all very impressive—quite the tourist spot."

"I can only imagine."

He raised a brow, reached into his pocket, pulled out a disc shaped spool, and placed its looped string around his finger.

"Stanford, what's that?" She squinted with curiosity.

"Call me Stan."

"Fine, *Stan*, but don't call me Ruth," she giggled. "What is it?"

He flipped his wrist as it rolled down the string and then rolled up, returning quickly to his hand.

"Amazing. It's like a sideways top. What do you call it?"

"You won't believe it."

"Try me."

"A yo-yo."

"You Americans—Piggy Wiggy stores and now a yo-yo." She eyed the interesting toy. "Can I try?"

He laughed and replied, "Certainly, give me your hand."

Perspiration immediately formed on her palm. This man was now holding her hand and placing the yo-yo string on her finger. In her opinion—nothing could be more romantic.

"This is an example of my means to a

prosperous future," he murmured.

"A yo-yo?"

"Yes, I am a wholesaler of unusual inventions brought from the United States." He demonstrated how to snap her wrist to get the toy to rewind. "I started big with garage door openers and garbage disposals, but now I deal in smaller items such as, clip-on ties, ice cube trays and bug zappers."

"*Amazing.*" She looked at him with awe. *He* was truly amazing. Her delight of the meeting increased as he revealed more about himself.

"Later, I added staple removers, tape dispensers, and, if you will pardon me, toilet brushes," he laughed.

"Astonishing! You can actually make a living selling those things?"

"Of course, they are all the rage."

Marvin's greeting cut her yo-yo lesson short. "Well, what have we here?"

Stanford jumped from the bench and ran to embrace his former colleague.

"Yo, Stan—old man! Mitt Me, kid!"

"Of course, congratulations, Marv. Sorry that I missed the happy event; I met the lucky lady an hour ago. She's quite a catch." He shook Marvin's hand.

"I know. Is she here? Oh, Hello, Ruthia."

"Marvin," she greeted him, smiling shyly, as if to hide her new secret admiration for his friend.

"No, your lovely bride left word that she's paying a short visit to her family," Stanford explained.

"Using the old yo-yo trick, eh Stan?"

Stanford shook his head disapprovingly. "Ignore the egg, Ruthia."

"I suppose that I should be getting back.' She left the bench. "I'm sure you two have a lot of catching up to do." She handed Stan the yo-yo.

"No, it's yours to keep. Next time I will teach you how to go 'around the world' or 'walk the dog.'"

"What?" Confused, she looked to Marvin for assistance.

"Tricks, Ruthia...with the yo-yo," he explained.

Ruthia blushed. "Yes, well, you two have a nice afternoon. Say 'hello' to Jeanie for me." She looked up to Stan. "I'm looking forward to our next visit...soon, I hope."

"Sooner than you think, Miss Sierzik," he replied, grinning. "Drive carefully."

Ruthia floated out of the Strickland garden, and then raced to the car. She hopped in and sped down the road. *Drive carefully.* So protective, just like her Uncle Hiram. Her fondest memory was of her ninth birthday. She and Zanya had received matching dresses—hers three sizes larger, but that wasn't big enough; she had popped off two buttons in preparing for the dreaded modeling to the clan. In her rage, she made an irreparable split to the skirt with her mother's scissors to avoid wearing it. In the midst of her feeble explanation, Hiram quickly covered for her and whisked her away to the mercantile to accompany him in picking up a supposed order.

Now, she had found another protector and self-made man like her Uncle. Well, Hiram could have been, had he not inherited all that money. In addition, Stanford was well travelled—the perfect companion. He met all the criteria to help her reach her goals in life— to be the wife of a handsome wealthy man, to entertain guests with elaborate parties, and to travel extensively while wearing the latest fashions. More importantly, she felt comfortable with him. She enjoyed listening to him. He seemed to enjoy talking to her and explaining things that she did not understand. He shared the details of his life during their very *first* visit. He did not mind her questions. He made her feel glad that she *was* Ruthia Sierzik; few in her life had made her feel confident in herself. His frankness made her feel that she in turn could confide in him. This was a promising match.

"*Mrs. Ruthia Seton,*" she repeated several times as she drove down the road to McDonnally Manor. Although she arrived home without the sketchbook, she was given a temporary reprieve—Zanya accepted Wilmoth's last minute request for "nanny duty" at their home for their baby, so she could accompany her husband on a job interview trip.

Three days had passed since Ruthia had visited the Strickland home; Mr. Seton had not attempted to contact her. Each morning she rose early, dressed, preparing for his expected arrival. Each passing hour left her anxious and despondent. Where was he? What if he never contacted her, again? She parked herself by the telephone, ready to respond to that thrilling ring. But, all was quiet in the Sierziks'. As night grew near, her hopes faded with the setting sun. Another day had passed without word from him. She panicked. *Maybe he was ill?* Or perhaps he was called away unexpectedly to America. Was he gone forever? She may never see him again! Her mood swung from sadness to concern for his well-being, to sheer disappointment. Then the anger set in; she was angry with him and angry with herself for being so foolish to trust him. It was time to cut her losses to keep her pride intact. She glared at the yo-yo clenched in her hand. "My life will go on happily and unscathed without you Mr. Stanford Seton."

At that very moment, Miles announced his arrival.

Chapter 9

"The Future?"

"Security is mostly a superstition. Life is either a daring adventure or nothing."

—Helen Keller

Since Ruthia was forbidden to leave the property with the gentleman, seven years her senior, Ruthia graciously accompanied him in a stroll around the grounds.

"So, Miss Ruthia, did you amaze your siblings with your new toy?"

"No...not yet." She dared not say anything to her family about him, for fear she would make a fool of herself.

"Not yet?"

"Oh, I will. My sister Zanya has gone away ...for a while."

"I'm just teasing. So, beautiful lady, what have you been up to, these last few days?" He took her hand in his and led her towards the garden.

She stared straight ahead, speechless. What could she say? She was not about to tell him the truth that she had been worried sick that she may never see him again or that she had wasted each day, pining for him, sitting by the phone like a pretty but useless and ultimately unnoticed, lace doily. So, she did what any other woman in this situation would do.

"What have *you* been up to?" she asked.

"Me? Missing you and wishing that Marvin would have invited someone else to accompany him to check out that piece of property." He dropped her hand and placed his left arm around her. The perfect fit. Had she been any shorter or taller it would have been awkward.

She smiled comfortably in his embrace, as they continued toward the garden.

"Property?" she inquired.

He put his right index finger to his lips. "Sh. It's a secret—Marvin's looking for land to build Jeanie a home. She cannot imagine living in the family home. She wants one of their own."

"So you have been travelling."

"So to speak, and yes, I'm glad to be back. I discovered that I find it very difficult to be away from you, Miss Sierzik, even though we just met. It was like someone had taken the sunshine away."

"Well, it has been raining since we last met," she giggled.

"Ruthia, I adore you." He squeezed her shoulder, grinning. She eased slowly into his embrace.

"You never answered my question. What has occupied your time, since you didn't have to put up with me and your sister's been away?"

"I missed you," she said, closely watching for his reaction.

"That's nice to hear." He smiled down at her and guided her to the stone bench.

Finally, she felt more relaxed and so comfortable, that she decided to confide in him.

"Stanford I'd like share something with you...something just between the two of us—a problem."

"You're not secretly married, are you?"

She laughed. "Heaven's no."

He squeezed her hand. His face grew serious. "I'm here to listen. Tell me what's troubling you."

"I'm in a pickle. It's really not my fault—I was robbed!" She removed her hand from his and folded hers in her lap.

"Robbed?" His brows rose.

"Yes," she sighed, "and I need cash, fast."

"Ruthia, that's nothing to worry about. I can give you a temporary loan. What are friends for, if not to bail them out of a dire situation?"

"No, no, I couldn't and wouldn't impose. You barely know me. You misunderstand. I just wanted to know if I could work for you for a while—bookkeeping or something—just until I made enough money to pay off a debt."

"Darling, I'm not about to become your employer. I will loan you the cash. I know you well enough to trust you implicitly." He cupped her face in his hands and leaned toward her as his eyes closed. His lips met hers, ever so gently. He opened his eyes and whispered, "I've been waiting to do that, since the first we met. Now, sweet girl, how much do you need?"

Ruthia was now dually content: floating on cloud nine in this new relationship and being prepared to satisfy her debt to Von and Zanya.

However, the fact that she still owed Stan was unacceptable.

Haunted by the money missing from Grandma Amanda's room, she decided to make one final attempt to find it. She rushed to the third floor, turned the key with the green tassel and entered the dark room, guided by her flashlight. Back to the glovebox, then to the jewelry box. This was ridiculous. She felt sure that it was not there. She was certain that Twyla had stolen it and had already spent it. But how could she ever prove it? Her new beau would be appalled. She felt certain that he would never let Twyla get away with it.

Discouraged and disheartened, Ruthia retreated to the vanity bench. She lighted her likeness in the mirror and stared at it. How could this happen to her, when everything else was going so well? She shone the beam on her the matronly portrait of Amanda, her great-grandmother. Suddenly, remorse set in. What had she done?

"Great Grandma, I truly am sorry for shaming the clan. It was a despicable thing to do. Please, forgive me." She reached for the drawer pull, opened the drawer, and reached in for a hankie. She removed a white one with coral tatted edges, dabbed her burning eyes and wiped her sniffling nose.

She reached in the drawer for another when her fingers touched something crisp, smooth, and entirely not hanky-like...She guided the beam of the light to the drawer. Her jaw dropped. It was a miracle! The money was back! She quickly, counted it. All six-hundred was there. She searched the drawer bottom in for more treasure. Okay, it *was* wishful thinking.

She withdrew her hand and examined the cash. She looked up at the portrait. "Oh, thank you, Grandma!"

She quickly placed her findings in her sweater pocket and started for the door. She paused and reconsidered. She must have overlooked it in her panic. Begrudgingly, she considered the possibility that she owed Twyla an apology, as well. On second thought, Twyla was undeserving; she had been unjustifiably rude to her.

At peace now, Ruthia rushed off to deliver the money to her father. She could barely wait to have the matter resolved, despite the fact that she would have only two-hundred pounds compared to her siblings three-hundred and fifty each. Finally, she could share her special secret with Zanya, when she returned. Ruthia had sorely missed her confidential talks with her sister and now there was so much to tell her.

Two hours later, Zanya arrived. Ruthia barely gave her two minutes to unpack, before crashing into her bedroom and bombarding her with the news.

"When I went to see Marvin, I met the most handsome man that ever walked the earth!"

"More handsome than Rufus?" Zanya asked dubiously.

"Heaven's yes. He's tall and blonde and—"

"More handsome than Great Uncle Hiram?" she taunted her.

Ruthia sat silent for a minute. "Yes, yes, yes!"

"That's fine but, did you happen to remember the purpose of your visit? Where's Von's sketchpad?"

"Oh *no*, I forgot all about it."

"How could you, Ruthia?"

"It could not be helped. I was so distracted."

"You'll have to go back. I'm not going to keep the truth from Von any longer."

"Oh, trust me, I will!"

"This boy must have really made an impression on you."

"He's not a boy and his name is Stanford Seton. I call him Stan. He calls me Ruthia. He has roots in Scotland, but he's an American."

"What is he doing here?"

"He was Marvin's flat mate in Edinburgh at the Business School. He had wanted to attend the wedding, but was delayed because of business."

"Hm? Wilmoth never mentioned anything

about him. What's his profession?" She raised a brow.

"He sells things—strange things—new inventions—wait here!" She ran out of the room.

A minute later, she returned with her prize yo-yo. "Watch!"

She demonstrated how it rolled down the string and returned to her palm.

"He actually survives on an income selling these?" Zanya cocked her head in doubt.

"Oh yes and more. Let's see." She put her finger to her head trying to remember. "Uh...bug dispensers..."

"Bug dispensers?" Zanya asked in disbelief.

"Yes. Perhaps for pet lizards or frogs...and toilet...trays.

Zanya scowled.

"Probably so you can eat while you—"

"Ruthia, that's disgusting!"

"Never mind that. He also sells yo-yos, clip-on ties and brush removers."

"What's a brush remover?"

"You know...for kids like Ivy. She gets her hairbrush tangled in her hair—this will probably remove it."

"How does that work?" Zanya squinted.

"How should I know? He used to sell garbage openers, too."

Her sister wrinkled her nose. "I'm not even going to ask." She propped the pillow behind her and leaned back. "Ruthie, he sounds strange."

"He's not strange—he's wonderful and well-travelled! He's been to Peru and has an authentic Incan poncho!"

"Why Peru?"

"Just touring, I guess. Why he even—" She stopped short; she had better not mention the loan. "He's going to teach me yo-yo tricks!"

"No, Ruthia, he's *not* strange...he's..." she trailed off. *He is nuts,* she thought. "Go to bed Ruthia. It is late. Oh, and don't forget to get the sketchbook from Marvin."

Ruthia placed no stock in her sister's opinion about Stanford, but so wanted to tell her about the kiss; there would be time for that later, after Zanya knew him better. Nothing was going to color Ruthia's love for the American. He brought a new light into her life. He was interested in her and *not* because she was a member of the McDonnally clan. He enjoyed being with her. *He had missed her.* He had called her "beautiful" and her size was no longer a worry to her. He included her in his future; her own parents were never remotely concerned about her life in the years to come, not like they were with Von and Zanya. She now felt like a woman for the first time in her life—a woman with great possibilities. She had met an older man that not only admired her, but also trusted her. Stanford Seton was now the most important person in her life because he made *her* feel important.

She glanced back at her reflection in the mirror. She was content. All was right with the world; her siblings were paid and speaking to her. She could even reimburse Stan. She opened the pearl beaded purse that lay on the table and slowly removed the £400 that Stan had loaned her. Oh, what she could do with this—especially, since she had had to forfeit her first hundred pounds to Von and Zanya as her punishment. Stan did not say exactly *when* she needed to pay him, perhaps never. Maybe they would marry and it would be silly for her to repay him. It would not hurt to wait. If they parted ways, God forbid, she would pay him…in installments; nowadays, everyone accepted installment plans.

She made the decision; she would use the loan to purchase a new wardrobe for the Paris trip. After all, she had to look stunning—Stan might very well accompany her.

Shortly thereafter, Ruthia returned to the Strickland home to inquire about her brother's sketchbook. To her disappointment, Stan was gone with Conrad for the day. Marvin explained to her that after confiscating the sketchbook from the boys at the party, he had indeed brought it home. However, he had honestly not seen it since the night of the birthday celebration. Ruthia returned home and reported her findings about the missing article, or lack of them, to her thoroughly disappointed sister. Her brother's privacy had been compromised, but there was nothing she could do, now.

The day had finally arrived for the Sierziks to send their only son out into the world, albeit reluctantly. Kade would accompany him. Before the sendoff, Von privately approached Ruthia.

"You saw my sketches. Where are they? I want to take them with me," he said firmly.

"I don't have them, Von. Yes, I saw them, but I swear that I would give them to you, if I had them. I don't know where they are, nor does anyone else. They have just disappeared. I'm so very sorry. Please, believe me." Her eyes teared up.

Von stared at her, then nodded and continued out to the driveway.

After a great deal of advice and fore-warnings from his parents, Von slid behind the wheel. His farewells were difficult, but the tears and silence of his youngest sister, Ivy was unbearable. Von and Ivy, joined at the hip, much like Rufus and Phemia, were always conversing and comforting one another. Ivy found little consolation in Von's promise to correspond with her and assurance that he would be returning in three short months to visit. Three months was an eternity to one so young.

A final wave from the aspiring young fashion designer left his mother sobbing and his father's brow rose. Zanya noted Ruthia smiling sincerely at Von. Could it be that Ruthia, now content with her life, actually wanted the same for her brother? Zanya swelled with pride of a sister to one so talented, waved, imagining his future success. From the corner of her eye, she saw Ivy rushing away, probably seeking privacy for a much-needed cry.

A few yards away, the McDonnally farewell for Kade was equally touching; teary-eyed Livia handed him a lunch pail and promised to write every week. Hiram gave him a proud pat on the back and a handshake for good luck. The twins vowed to visit within a few months.

The two young men were off for London and a new future—or so it was believed. To Von's surprise after only two miles, Kade asked Von to stop the car. He got out, saying only, "I'll explain later."

Kade—"Thomas Kade" named for his father killed in the war, was Von's best friend. They had grown up together. Kade was the popular one at school—excellent cricket player, promising architect. Everyone was drawn to him, but he chose to keep his life private. Von had learned early on, not to pry.

Kade would share his feelings and thoughts when he was ready. Kade had once confessed to him that the best day in his life was the day the twins, Amanda and Alex were born. For the first time he felt part of a real family and no longer so alone. He swore that someday he would have a whole parcel of bairns. Von, being the only male in a set of triplets, thought this plan was ludicrous.

Even so, Von respected his friend, so if Kade said he would explain his departure later, Von would just have to wait. His thoughts returned to his conversation with Ruthia. He had to believe that she truly did not know the whereabouts of his sketchbook. But where was it?

Von had visited London on several occasions with his family, but had never ventured away from Lochmoor Glen on his own. The spirit of a new life was upon him in every aspect. Von mentally absorbed his surroundings, from a new perspective—this would be his *home*. His only fear was that of meeting his new mentor. She was a woman with a flawless character, phenomenal talent, and a spotless reputation. He had never seen her likeness, but rumor was that she was particularly easy on the eyes and quite well preserved.

His stride quickened as he approached his temporary residence at the Midland Grand

Hotel. He smiled with satisfaction, at the recently renovated St. Pancras area—the slums were cleared out, eliminating the rat and lice problems at the hotel. He would soon begin his search for a flat in close proximity to hers, where she had the art studio. He was to meet her the next day for dinner. Until then, he would familiarize himself with the neighborhood. He was particularly eager to visit the art store to inspect the coveted supplies of every true artist in Town.

After his shopping spree, he returned to his room, fully equipped to begin his new career. He could not help but wonder where Kade's change in plans had led him.

That evening in the McDonnally Manor dining room, Zanya asked Ivy, "Little sister, are you up for an evening ride to Duncan Ridge?"

Ivy paused in the middle of eating a bite of potato. "It...it's awfully chilly."

Sophia immediately cut in, "Ivy are you catching a cold?"

"Maybe, Mama," she mumbled.

"Then you had better decline the invitation," Sophia insisted.

Ivy smiled. Her belief that the missing horses would not be discovered, was short-lived.

Ruthia promptly spoke up, "Stan's busy with Conrad this evening, so I'll go."

"Great!" Zanya agreed. "Give me a few minutes when we're finished here. I want to get my new riding boots."

"It's about time that you broke them in. A wise choice for your gift money," Sophia noted proudly.

Ivy's anxiety immediately increased twofold when Miles delivered a note to her great uncle Hiram, seated at the head of the table. She nervously scrutinized his alarmed expression, as he read it.

Livia touched his hand. "Darling, what is it?"

"I'm not sure. I have to go to Brachney Hall."

"I'll have Twyla save you some afters."

He nodded absent-mindedly. "Please bring my motorcar around, Miles."

Ivy sank down in her chair.

Hiram arrived to find Naomi pacing in the drawing room.

"Hiram, you have to do something! Edward left here like a madman!"

"*Nomi*, calm down. Gone where?"

"He's gone to confront Rufus!"

"Why Rufus?"

"Smitty is missing. She's been gone all day. She said that she was spending the day with Ivy, but I met Allison at the mercantile. Ivy has been with *Addison* all day—not Smitty."

"What has all this to do with Rufus?"

"At the birthday party, Smitty was missing there, too. We believe that she was with Rufus. Hiram, Edward's livid and not thinking straight. Please go to the Dugan's!"

"I'm on my way. Relax and... have some tea or something."

"Thank you. Please *hurry*."

The scene at the Dugan's was not one Lochmoor Glen residents would soon lay to rest. Even with the two greatest gossipers now residing in London, the rumors made their way across the moors in record time—thanks to the telephone, even Harriet Dugan got in her two cents.

As recounted, Edward had arrived at the Dugan cottage where he had met Tavy, Rufus's adoptive father. Despite the two men's past friendship, Edward had made some unsavory accusations about Rufus, whereupon Tavy had instinctively retaliated with his fist.

One black eye later, Rufus had shown up with Miss Dara Wheaton on his arm with the intention of showing her his donkey, Pete.

Rufus had helped Edward to his feet, while Edward awkwardly apologized. Hiram then quickly rescued Edward from further embarrassment with an invitation to escort him home.

"Edward, let's stop at my home and put a beefsteak on that eye, before it swells shut."

Edward nodded.

When they entered the kitchen at McDonnally Manor, they discovered an escalating exchange between Zanya and Ivy. Ruthia was trying to referee, but was failing in her attempts.

"How dare you take them without my permission?" Zanya screeched.

"It was not my idea!" Ivy countered.

"Take who?" Hiram asked.

"Whose idea was it then, the *horses*?" Zanya refuted.

"No, of course not!" Ivy shouted.

"What idea?" Hiram intervened, again, without notice.

"Ivy, if anything has happened to them, I will never forgive you!" Zanya glanced up at her great uncle. "Uncle Edward! What happened to you?" she asked, shocked out of her rage.

Ivy and Ruthia followed suit, "Have you been in a brawl?"

Edward shook his head. "Get me out of here, Hiram."

Hiram grabbed a beefsteak from the icebox and handed it to Edward. The two left slowly down the corridor. The argument ensued.

"They're my horses! Who has them?" Zanya demanded.

Hiram and Edward continued to the car and drove to Brachney Hall, where Edward attempted to explain the events at the Dugan cottage. It was not until Naomi asked the key question, that Hiram started putting it all together—or at least part of the puzzle.

She said, "I have been thinking. Do you think Ivy may know something? After all, Smitty did say that she was spending the day with her and then did not. They are as close as sisters."

Hiram narrowed his eyes. *"'They're my horses—who has them?'"* Hiram repeated mysteriously.

"What?" Naomi asked, wondering if Hiram was the one who was punchy.

He clarified, "Zanya and Ivy were arguing. Ivy had taken Baron and Hunter somewhere and gave them to someone, from what I understand."

This stirred the interest of the distraught parents.

"Smitty left on a horse?" Edward asked, obviously not himself.

Naomi took Hiram's arm. "Both horses are gone? Our Smitty has gone off with some-one...somewhere and Ivy's been sworn to secrecy. Good heavens, where? With whom?"

"Naomi," Hiram swallowed hard, "I think we had better have Jules put Edward to bed and go have a talk with Miss Ivy."

Chapter 10

"Lochmoor Glen Revisited"

"The years went by and never knew
That each one brought ne nearer you;
Their path was narrow and apart
And yet it led me to your heart—"

—Sara Teasdale

Twenty minutes later, Hiram and Naomi marched down the main hall of the manor like the troops ready to conquer.

"Ivy!" Hiram bellowed.

The chatter in the kitchen stopped.

Hiram and Naomi stood in the doorway.

Zanya was in near tears, "Ivy, I'm telling Mother and Father! They'll make you talk!"

She started for the hall when Hiram said to her, "No need for that, Zanya. Ivy, come with us to my study."

Ivy lowered her head and followed like a prisoner going to the gallows. Doom was certainly eminent. She stood before her accusers. Hiram began the questioning.

"Ivy, who has Zanya's horses?"

"I had to help them! No one would understand!"

"Help who?" Naomi asked fearfully.

"What else could they do? They're in *love*," Ivy pleaded.

"Who is in love?" Naomi panicked, grabbing Ivy by the shoulders.

Ivy started to cry. "I promised. I gave her my word!" She tightened her fists.

Naomi released her grasp.

"*Who*, Ivy?" Hiram insisted. "You have to tell us, now."

Ivy looked at them through a blur of tears.

"Who Ivy?" Naomi repeated, in frustration.

"Smitty."

"Dear Lord, help me. Ivy, who is with her?"

Naomi swallowed hard.
Ivy looked helplessly to Hiram.
"Who is the boy, Ivy?" he commanded.
Ivy took a breath. "Kade, sir."

Early that morning, a few minutes after Von had driven away in the vehicle, it *was* Smitty who had appeared riding Baron and leading Hunter,
"Right on time," Kade said, taking the reins and mounting Hunter.
"It went like clockwork," she murmured. "Ivy pretended to go to her room after the send-off, and then met me in the meadow with the horses. I took the shortcut through the moors and here I am."
"And your parents believe that you are spending the day with Ivy, as planned?"
"Yes...Ivy's spending the day with Addison, as Allison had errands to run."
"Well, Smitty, I guess all our bases are covered, as they would say in baseball. We'll bring a gift back for her for our appreciation. We'd better get going."
"Wait." She pulled back on the reins and glanced down at them. "Kade, are you *certain* that this is what you want?" He didn't respond, forcing her to look at him.
He moved his horse next to hers and leaned toward her. He pulled Smitty close, as his grip tightened on her shoulder. He kissed her, once softly and then again with the love of

a man who unquestionably was quite sure about what *he* wanted. They each took a breath and sat upright.

"Now, you *did* get the directions from Ivy, didn't you?" Kade asked.

She nodded. Sophia had been more than happy to enthrall her daughter with the full details of her elopement to the little village on the border. Smitty pointed down the road. "Straight ahead."

After Naomi and Hiram's interrogation of Miss Ivy, the facts were spread before both McDonnally couples. Smitty had eloped with Kade.

For Edward and Naomi, their baby girl of sixteen was much too young to enter a marriage. They had no objection to eighteen-year-old Kade as a future mate for their daughter; they loved him dearly. However, the operative word was "future." They were in shock. Hiram and Livia, likewise adored their niece Smitty, but Kade's future as a successful architect was compromised beyond repair. The young couple had left early that morning to be married. It was too late; the damage was done and no one could see the silver lining in this situation until Edward solemnly summed it up.

"Well, I would say that the joy in all this is that now we are all related...but we already were."

***

That night, Hiram and Livia lay wide-awake contemplating Kade's dismal future.

"Hiram, they'll have children and no income!"

"I thought I raised him better than this. I would have sworn that he had a good head on his shoulders. He is such a talented draftsman." He folded his arms across his chest.

Livia sat up with a start. "What if they have to come and live with us...with all those babies?"

"Edward is probably insane with panic for his daughter's future. He will probably blame me for not having the *talk* with Kade."

Her eyes widened. "You never talked to Kade about—uh!"

"Livy he's a grown man—a married man, now. It's a little late for the 'talk.'"

There was knocking at their door.

"Come in," Hiram replied.

Ivy peeked in. "I just wanted to apologize to you both for keeping the secret."

Livia said gently, "It is okay, Ivy. You are a woman of your word. That is a virtue. Go back to bed, Sweetie."

Hiram rolled his eyes.

There was another knock at the door.

"Come in, Ivy." He sighed.

Hiram and Livia smiled at one another.

The door opened.

"Mother, Father?"

Both sat up with a start.

"I have something to tell you," Kade said cautiously.

Neither parent spoke when he stepped inside the room.

"Today, Smitty and I went to...to be married."

"Blasted, Kade!" Hiram shouted. Livia grabbed his arm before he lunged from the bed.

"Hiram, hear him out!" She swallowed and said in a calm, controlled tone, "Go ahead, Kade."

"Thank you, Mother. As I was saying, we went without consulting anyone."

Except Ivy, they both thought.

"However, before Smitty consented to marrying me, she broke down and ran out," he reported with apparent disdain. "Against my better judgment, I spent hours trying to change her mind."

"Are you married?" Hiram demanded.

"No, Father."

Hiram raised his hands to the heavens, "Thank the Lord!"

"That's all I have to say. I'm sorry that I missed supper." Kade turned and left the room, closing the door behind him.

"*Sorry he missed supper?*" Hiram repeated. "Unbelievable."

"He's still growing. He's probably hungry," Livia said and scooted down beneath the covers. "I would have helped with all of those babies," she muttered, as she dozed off. "I wonder why she left him at the altar. No matter. At least *she* had some sense. I'll have to commend Edward on her upbringing."

Livia was right—Kade was hungry and made a beeline for the kitchen. He was surprised to find Ruthia sitting at the kitchen table at that late hour.

"Kade, you're back! Where's Smitty?" she said beaming for their joy.

"At home," he answered, removing the cake cover.

"Home? Shouldn't she be with you, her husband?"

"I'm not her husband. We were never married. At the last minute, she changed her mind. She wouldn't listen to me." He took a plate and fork from the pantry.

"I'm sorry. It was all so romantic—the two of you sneaking off to elope."

He lifted a piece of cake onto the plate and sat down across from her. "The romance is over. We won't be seeing each other anymore."

"I adore Smitty, but she is a twit—an absolute twit! Any woman would be thrilled at the idea of running away with one so handsome, kind and...intelligent as you."

He laid down his fork. "Intelligent? I'm the twit. Any woman? That's the problem. I should have known that she was a *lassie*, too young to go through with it."

Kade's response did not surprise Ruthia. Kade's pet peeve was indecisiveness. She had once planned a picnic with him and was having difficulty in deciding to bring either chicken or roast beef. He blew up and cancelled on her. That would have been their first and only outing together.

"Well. Kade, as they say, 'love is blind.' Cheer up. Have a bite of that cake. It's murder! Although, it may bring on a rash of nightmares, eating it at this hour," she laughed a little.

"Right now, I'm already living a nightmare. I've lost everything in one swoop—my girl, my career, my future, and my parents respect."

She reached for his wrist and looked at him with sincerity. "I respect you. You're not the only one who has made a major brodie. Stealing from my brother and my sister, didn't earn me any gold stars. At least you had a credible excuse. When you are in love, nothing else seems to matter—and it shouldn't. I commend you for acting on your feelings...if only Smitty would have." She wiped her mouth with her napkin. "I know all about love."

"You do?" he asked skeptically and took a bite.

"Yes, I have found the love of my life...I think. Stanford Seton."

"Seton?"

"Of course."

"I thought you blew your wig over Rufus. Especially, since he is available, now."

"Rufus is sweet—but Stan is so sophisticated, truly a man of the world."

"Does that make a man, in your opinion?" he asked casually.

"Why every woman desires to be seen on the arm of a highly successful, well-travelled man."

He shoved his chair back and stood up. "So that's it. I am anything but successful. Thanks for the information, Ruthia," he added spitefully and left.

His bitter response left her speechless. What had she done? Now, he was thoroughly depressed; she had made matters worse. She pushed her half-empty plate away.

"Ruthia, why don't you keep your big mouth shut," she muttered.

After a near sleepless night, Von set out to introduce himself to his new mentor. The meeting began awkwardly, but within minutes, the two were getting along quite famously.

"Madame—"

"Von you may call me Liza. I abhor formality with my students."

"Very well, Liza..." A long pause followed. Von's face reddened.

"Von, what's wrong?"

He swallowed hard— "I...I forgot what I was going to say," he muttered.

Her sweet voice and simple beauty was overwhelming. Yes, she was mature—much older than his mother was, but she was sophisticated and refined. He had never met anyone like her.

She laughed and placed her hand on his.

"You will soon discover that I am the one guilty of a short memory," she teased.

He relaxed and laughed with her. He studied her face.

"Von, tomorrow, I will show you my studio. The lighting is superb and the view is inspiring."

He noted that when she spoke, tiny dimples appeared at the corners of her mouth. Her eyes danced, only making contact with his for a brief half-second.

"I have several returning clients that periodically require a new design for a formal event," she explained.

As she humbly noted her success in the fashion industry, she cocked her head slightly, shyly, as though she was embarrassed to acknowledge her merit. Von immediately admired her lack of arrogance.

"Now, as for you young man, your work shows tremendous promise and uniqueness. With only a small degree of direction, I believe that you will be prepared to take on some of the workload. I know of at least three of my clients that will be fascinated by your creations." Her encouraging words were spoken with genuine sincerity.

Von felt a great sense of security embarking on this new career. Her tone initiated some confusion, though. She reminded him of someone. Who was it? Perhaps a past teacher...yes, his Sunday school teacher, Miss Giles. Oh, did he ever have a crush on her. She had placed a kiss on his forehead when she had presented him with the perfect attendance award. Oh, if she had only known that *she* was his only reason for never missing a class—well that, and his mother's threats.

Liza's melodious voice faded to a murmur as Von was lost in a cloud of anticipation at the idea of working daily with this angel.

"Von, Von?"

"Yes, I'm so sorry. I was thinking about...something."

"Sir, I invited you to dine with me. There is a lovely bistro not far from here. The food is always a delight."

Sir? He beamed. Yes, he was a man and she a woman...a bit older, but beautiful. He was confident, he was Von "manstrong" and Liza was sweet and sincere. He would trust his life with her. They may become best friends or perhaps more.

"It would be my pleasure, thank you." He leaned back in his chair and nodded, taking in the full view of her.

***

The weeks sped by in Lochmoor Glen. Kade and Smitty had not rekindled their relationship. Smitty had confessed that she wanted a real wedding someday and was not prepared to be anyone's wife, as yet. This put her parents at ease for the time being. After *her* blunder, Ruthia kept her distance from Kade, too—never speaking to him, only offering an occasional nod. It was not long before he returned to London to resume his position at the architectural firm.

As for Von, his drawing capabilities, regarded as quite advanced, now proved to be near expert and becoming more so with each passing day. Liza was thoroughly pleased, as his progress showed even more promise than anticipated. His creativity was unbounded. He designed a variety of fashions. Liza was bowled over by his casual, wide-lapelled, loose blouses with bold printed, high-waisted trousers. His floor-length evening attire, trimmed with silver fox, dazzled several customers. There was always a demand for his countless split tennis skirts; swimwear and professional suits with long, straight skirts and hip-length, belted jackets. Needless to say, Miss Clayton could not be more pleased with her new associate.

After hours, the young Mr. Sierzik, decked out in top hat, tie, and tails would escort his instructor to supper, the opera, and the theater. They had seen *Farewell to Arms* with Gary Cooper at the movies, spent evenings at the Royal Opera House, and they even attended a night at the grand opening of the New Shakespeare Memorial Theatre. However, despite his busy schedule, he always found time for a weekly post to his little sister. Ivy's letters read like the diary of a very atypical teenager. She made no mention of her peers, current fads, or crushes on the local lads. Instead, she wrote of village gossip, accounts of poetic ventures to the pond, tidbits from eavesdropping on the adults and her plans to monopolize her brother's visits.

Exactly three months after von left for London, Ivy shot down the hallway of the manor carrying the much-awaited letter—the one announcing his return to Lochmoor Glen.

Two days later, Miles, the honorable McDonnally butler, slowly worked his way to answer the countless raps of the doorknocker in his usual stately manor. However, upon opening the door to the jovial countenance of his beloved Von, he lost all control and moved quickly in to hug the young man who he had cherished since infancy.

"Master Von, 'tis grand to see you! We did not expect to see you for another two days."

"With the new highway roads and automobiles, we made the trip in a flash."

"And who do I have the pleasure of

announcing?" He looked to the lovely woman standing quietly next to Von. The butler's brows rose and he swallowed. "W...welcome, Madame."

At that moment, Hiram came out of his study, asking, "What's all the commotion?" He looked toward his great nephew. "Von, my lad, you're back and looking quite—" His gaze fell upon Von's guest. His jaw dropped.

Von glanced curiously at his great uncle, then at Liza.

Hiram mumbled, "Elizabeth?"

She reached for his hand. "Hello, Hiram. How are you?"

"Me? I...I am well."

Von turned to her. "You know him?"

"Yes, we met in Town many years ago."

Seeking some assistance, Hiram turned awkwardly to the butler. "Miles, invite them into the parlor, well her, I mean them—Von lives here...uh, I'll inform the others." Hiram started to leave, but the gravity of the situation kept him from moving. He was awestruck; there she was—Elizabeth Clayton in his home, once again. Only this time she was on the arm of his very young, great nephew who was apparently attempting to look much older by wearing a newly acquired, dapper, pencil-thin mustache.

Elizabeth had barely changed physically, except for the few strands of silver framing her face. She was still very beautiful. However, her chic, cultured manner was unfamiliar.

Prior to Hiram and Livia being reunited, Hiram had met Miss Clayton at an art exhibit. He had tried desperately to become better acquainted with her, but she ultimately had rejected his advances, feeling that her poor station in life as a starving artist was not compatible with his lifestyle. Their relationship had ended abruptly and bitterly. Later, Elizabeth had sent a piece of her pottery, a cup, as a means to mend the broken relationship. It had been all for naught—Hiram had had no desire to renew their association.

Miss Clayton's return was anything but awkward for the other family members. Elizabeth was still very personable with an angelic face to match. It was not until Livia excused herself to speak with Miles in the front hall that she discovered the reason for the familiarity with the guest.

Livia returned to the parlor, focused on Von's stunning travelling companion—Hiram's former "sweetheart." Miss Clayton was taller than she was and apparently about the same age. Her smile was innocent and unbearably sweet. Yes, she could imagine Hiram being attracted to her. But she was travelling with Von—a *very* young man. Why was she *really* here? Did she still have feelings for Hiram? Was she using Von?

Livia's thoughts were cut short when Sophia commented, "Miss Clayton, I would wager that you were shocked when you entered the drive."

Elizabeth replied, "Actually, Von had mentioned Lochmoor Glen when we first met. I naturally assumed that he was acquainted with the McDonnallys—though not that he was actually a family member," she laughed a little.

Livia did not. She slowly turned to her husband's fixed gaze on Elizabeth; it was as though he was in a trance—confused by the entire situation.

Von sat up straight. "Liza has been an incredible mentor. I've learned a great deal in such a short time."

"Thank you, Von, but his talents require very little polishing. He has a plethora of unique designs stored away in that creative brain. He can't seem to get them down on paper quickly enough!" Liza added.

Von's father, Rahzvon, appeared to be smiling all too attentively at the tall, lovely guest, as well. Sophia, apparently disturbed by his indiscreet interest in the guest, quickly redirected the conversation towards her.

"Von, have you designed an outfit for your loving mother?"

"Yes, Mother, I have. I have the sketches with me. I chose fabric with vertical lines to make you look taller and more slender!"

Livia watched as Sophia's eyes widened; her brows furrowed.

Von panicked, "Not that you are too short, Mother, or too heavy—"

Rahzvon jumped in, "I'm certain that your sketches are perfect...especially if Miss Clayton gave her stamp of approval." This cheery compliment obviously did little to appease Sophia; it only enraged her—as was apparent by the way she smoothed her skirt with a number of vicious strokes. Von, on the other hand, smiled, notably pleased that his father had finally commented positively about his change in career.

Livia took that opportune moment of silence to glean an answer to the question nagging her.

"Von, how long shall we have the pleasure of your company?" she asked. She dare not make eye contact with Liza.

"For only a few days, I'm afraid."

Sophia responded in a melancholy tone, "Only a few days?"

Hiram spoke for the first time since he had greeted them in the front hall. For Livia, life would have been better, had he chosen not to, especially since his inquiry was directed to Miss Clayton. "Oh no...must you go so soon?"

Elizabeth glanced around the room at the family. All were seemingly speechless at the unexpected plea. "Sorry, but we have a tremendous amount of work left to do. Von and I have to meet a deadline for a Town fashion show."

Livia's stomach began to turn. This could be the longest "few" days of her life. Von took his guest's hand in his.

"I think Liza and I would like to get settled in our rooms before we dine."

"Of course," Hiram spoke up and rang for Miles. "I shall see you in an hour, then," he added and excused himself to his study.

As the travelers left the room, Livia turned to Sophia. "Your son seems to be doing well."

"Too well," she said through clenched teeth.

Rahzvon objected, "Why do you say that?"

"You do have eyes, don't you?"

"Yes, I do," he answered, smiling broadly.

His unappreciated grin melted away with Sophia's fiery glare. "You need to speak with him, Rahzvon," her sharp tongue announced.

"About what?" he asked.

"His apparent infatuation with Miss Clayton. Great Scott, she's as old as Livia!"

Livia cocked her head in disapproval.

"I meant nothing, dergatory, Livia."

"*Derogatory*, Phia," Rahzvon whispered.

"No matter. Miss Clayton is not romantically interested in him and he should *not* be interested in her—she is older than his mother!"

"Phia, don't be ridiculous. She is his teacher. I'm sure that he just has the utmost respect for her and admiration for her artistic talents."

"Mr. Sierzik, your son has admiration for her, but not for her *artistic* talent! A mother knows her son. You have to warn him before his heart is broken! You need to speak to him tonight, directly after supper. He needs to socialize with girls his own age."

"I will not embarrass the boy with invalid precautions!" He said, shaking his finger at her.

She pushed his finger down. "First of all, Von will not be embarrassed. He is obviously independent and open-minded. Secondly, he is not a boy; he is an easily influenced man...like his *father*. Thirdly, there is nothing invalid about his behavior. Mark my words! Now, I must take a nap. This entire ordeal has exhausted me." She left to retire.

Rahzvon turned to Livia. "Sorry about that."

"How well do you know Miss Clayton?"

"I don't. I wasn't here, then. That was BC—before the clan," he laughed. "My loss." He got up to leave. "I will see you later."

Livia stood alone in the room. All sense of security as Mistress of the estate had fled. The fact that: she had been married to Hiram for years, had adopted Kade with him, and had given birth to their twins was of no consolation. He was feeling something for Miss Clayton. Part of Livia wanted to know what he felt; the other part was terrified of the possibilities.

***

Dinner was a gathering of much laughter and gaiety; Ivy saw to that. Ruthia sat quietly in the background. She felt that Von still held her responsible for the missing sketchbook. The rule that "children should be seen and not heard" was unanimously *overruled*. Ivy's silly anecdotes regarding Life in Lochmoor Glen and philosophical notions left no moment for boredom.

"Now, I ask *you* Miss Clayton—Von had no answer for me—if you speak to a dog in two different or even five different languages, can it understand you? And if you speak to it in French and you take it to Paris will it understand the natives?"

Elizabeth burst out laughing, "Ivy, you definitely have your brother's imagination!"

"Ivy, eat your dinner and leave our guest to enjoy hers," Rahzvon insisted.

"Mr. Sierzik, I don't mind, I think her questions are delightful. Ivy, in my opinion, dogs tend to understand body language, as well as spoken language."

"Body language?" Ivy asked.

"Yes, expressions, gestures, and the like. Dogs appear to understand verbal commands but the human tone of voice surely plays apart, too."

Livia raised a brow. *Such an* expert.

Hiram put down his fork. "Aye, I had a dog, God rest her soul—Gantwell, understood my feelings, from the moment that she entered the room."

"Yes," Elizabeth agreed, "dogs, cats and even horses are intuitive to our emotions."

Hiram nodded. "Hunter and I have had an incredible bond."

"You still have Hunter?" Elizabeth asked excitedly.

"Aye, but now he belongs to Zanya." Zanya offered a proud grin.

"I'd love to see him again and Duff too!"

"Elizabeth, we lost Duff a few years ago." Hiram said gently.

Her smile faded. "I'm sorry. He was a magnificent horse."

"If Zanya wouldn't mind, I'll take you to see Hunter when we are finished eating," Hiram offered hastily.

Zanya agreed, "Certainly. I have an appointment with Martha, anyway."

"Very well, we will head down to the stables after the afters," Hiram chuckled.

Livia bit her bottom lip and slowly turned toward the twins. "Children, it is late. Go straight to bed after you finish your dessert."

"Yes, Mama," they replied in unison.

Distracted by Von's beaming at Elizabeth while she thanked Twyla for the delicious meal, Hiram made no response to Livia's instructions. Hiram was not the only one who noticed Von's interest in Elizabeth. Sophia nudged Rahzvon and nodded at him. He rolled his eyes and sighed.

"Son, may I please have a word with you while Hiram is entertaining Miss Clayton?"

Entertaining? Livia cringed at the thought.

"Of course, Father." He nodded at Rahzvon.

Hiram and Elizabeth were laughing as they headed toward the backdoor. Livia scooted the twins upstairs. Her heart sank when Elizabeth, very naturally, took Hiram's arm—*body language* that Livia could have done without.

"So, you gave up pottery," Hiram commented.

"Oh, yes, years ago," Elizabeth laughed.

Chapter 11

"Temporary Insanity"

"Love is one who enters someone's heart,
even if it is taboo."

—Tsonga proverb

Meanwhile, Rahzvon and Von borrowed Hiram's study for their private conversation. Rahzvon was closing the pocket doors when Von asked, "Father, what is it?"

"Nothing, really—it is your mother."

"Mother? She's not ill?" he panicked.

"No...no." He shook his head, looking to the floor.

"She's not having another child?"

"Absolutely not...Son, she's concerned about your social life." He tightened his lips and raised his brows.

"My *social* life?"

"She just needs reassurance that you're dating...er, not working all the time."

"Oh, is that all." He patted his father's shoulder and walked toward the door. "Tell her that there is no need to worry about that—I have Miss Clayton!" He smiled and opened the doors. "I promised Ivy that I would see her latest creation. Good night, Father."

The bewildered parent stood there speechless.

After a long meditative stroll down the drive, Rahzvon retired to the East Wing. He stealthily entered the master bedroom in hopes of not waking Sophia. However, his curious wife lay in wait.

"Did you speak with Von?" she asked, startling him.

Rahzvon removed his boots, undressed,

slipped on his nightshirt, and slid into bed beside her.

"Yes, I did."

"How did he respond?"

"He said to tell you not to worry."

"About?"

"About his social life...dating young women."

She sat up. "So, he is not interested in Miss Clayton?" she asked skeptically.

Rahzvon did not want to lie to his wife, but reporting the truth would definitely have dire consequences. Sophia was no fool; she would probably detect Von's obsession with Miss Clayton, the very next time that she saw them together.

"Phia, Von's a grown man—er, nearly. He has to make his own choices and his own mistakes."

She flew out from under the covers.

"He is in love with her and *you* said nothing to forbid it!" She left the bed. "My poor baby! Why didn't you warn him?" she screeched.

"Sh! You'll wake up the whole house. Phia, I tried, but he left to talk to Ivy before I had a chance. You are close to him. You talk to him."

"Mr. Sierzik, he is your only son. He shan't listen to *my* advice about another woman. You go find him right now, before it's too late and he makes a fool of himself and proposes...or worse!"

He whipped off his nightshirt, pulled on his trousers and shirt, snatched up his boots and left, slamming the door behind him. He descended the stairs, mumbling as he entered the main hall, and sat down on the bench and pulled on his boots. Grimacing, he started toward the kitchen where he found Livia alone, standing at the window.

"Livia?"

Startled, she jumped. "Rahzvon...I was waiting for Hiram. I thought that you had retired for the evening."

"I did, but Phia is on the warpath."

"About what...if I may ask."

"Miss Clayton."

Livia took a seat at the table and made no reply. He sat down across from her.

"Phia suspects that Von is 'preoccupied' with his teacher." He reached for a biscuit on the plate in front of him.

"He is."

"I know—he confessed to me. Phia wants me to nip it in the bud—convince Von to abandon any notion of a serious relationship with her."

At that moment, Von and Ivy shot passed the kitchen, the backdoor slamming behind them.

Rahzvon swallowed. "There he goes. He can't leave her out of his sight for long." He took another bite. "What should I do?"

"That's between you and Sophia. You are

his parents." On the one hand, she, too, was concerned for Von; Elizabeth was entirely too old for him; he could be deeply hurt. On the other hand, if Von lost interest in her, Hiram may pick up the slack. "Perhaps, it would be best to be honest with him after they return to London, so as not to cast a shadow over their visit."

Livia took a cookie and ate it with no knowledge as to what kind it was. She and Rahzvon sat in silence until Liza, Von, and Ivy paused at the doorway and said goodnight. Ivy ran to her father and gave him a kiss and a hug.

Hiram then entered alone, smiling like a Cheshire cat. "Having a late night snack?" he addressed them and helped himself to a biscuit, as well. "Elizabeth could not believe how well Hunter looked after all these years."

"Did you show her Baron—my gift from *you*?" Livia asked.

"No, he was out grazing. What are you doing down here at this hour, Mr. Sierzik? Another bout with my niece?" he laughed.

"Actually, yes."

"What's the bee in her bonnet this time?" Hiram teased.

Livy held her breath for fear of the forthcoming direction of the conversation. Her fears were well founded.

"Phia is concerned about—I am, as well. Von is entirely *too* interested in Miss Clayton."

"Interested?" Hiram grinned.

"Romantically," Rahzvon clarified.

"Romantically? Don't be ridiculous. Von's but a lad—he's only seventeen. You both have over-active imaginations. He merely admires her abilities." He took another biscuit.

"No, Hiram. Von admitted to me that...he is drawn to her."

"Well, that is only natural—we all are."

Livia felt her rage brewing.

Rahzvon left his chair. "Hiram, he is interested in a woman older than his mother— nearly old enough to be his grandmother!"

Livia quickly took the opportunity to draw out Hiram's true colors and added, "Perhaps it's mutual."

They turned to her, glaring.

She continued, "It is not uncommon for a mature woman to desire the company of a much younger man."

That comment rang the bell to start the yelling match between the two enraged men.

"I shan't have it! You get control of your son!" Hiram yelled, slamming the biscuit to the table.

"My son will not continue working for a woman...like that!"

"What do you mean, 'a woman like that'?" Hiram countered, moving into his opponent's face.

"A woman who—"

"I'll hear no more of this! Elizabeth is an

honorable woman. It is your son who is out of line!"

Livia was livid as her husband fought to defend Miss Clayton's integrity.

"Von is an innocent boy with no knowledge of females with agendas!" Rahzvon countered, standing tall, glaring.

"How dare you suggest that Elizabeth has ulterior motives!"

"She came here to your house to meet his family! Deny that, Hiram!" He shook his finger at him.

"She may have other reasons for visiting!"

"Such as?" Rahzvon probed, thrusting his hands to his hips.

"To see me!"

"To see *you?*" Rahzvon squinted in disbelief.

"Elizabeth and I are not strangers, Mr. Sierzik!"

For Livia, that remark was the last straw; she could not leave her seat quickly enough. She removed herself from the room unnoticed, as the verbal battle continued.

Breakfast the next morning was quiet after the argument of the night before. Ivy had joined Zanya on a ride to Brachney Hall for breakfast with Smitty. Amanda and Alexander followed for a fishing trip at the pond. Livia welcomed this chance to avoid their exposure to the family tension. Von and Ruthia were the only members of the younger generation to be present.

Sophia and Rahzvon were not speaking to each other. Livia was not speaking to Hiram, but he was not aware of it. He had not spoken to her since his run-in with Rahzvon. Initially, Von and Liza were oblivious to the tension.

Then Von announced, "It seems that, you will not be the only Sierzik present at the Paris Fashion Show, Ruthia."

Her eyes widened. "You're going?"

Von reached over and touched Liza's hand. "Thanks to my gracious mentor, we are."

This gesture nearly catapulted Rahzvon and Hiram from their chairs. Sophia glared at Rahzvon. Hiram's brows furrowed.

"How positively perfect!" Ruthia exclaimed. "Now, Stan and I can go together—Von can chaperone!"

Sophia began to wilt—both of her children in the company of ill-suited partners?

Von cut in, "Hold on, Ruthia! Who invited you?"

Elizabeth spoke up, "Von, it might be fun—the four of us."

"Fun" was not a word that Sophia was comfortable with, but "four" meant safety in numbers.

Sophia smiled weakly. "Since Ruthia has tickets and she cannot attend alone with Mr. Seton, I suppose it would be for the best."

"But Mother!" Von objected.

"Von, it will be fine. Not to worry, Mrs. Sierzik." Elizabeth confirmed.

Not to worry? Sophia looked away when she read the pleased countenance on her son's face.

"If you think that it's a good idea, Liza. We will all go together and look after her," Von said, looking longingly at her hand beneath his.

At this, Hiram excused himself and left the room. Rahzvon followed suit. The remaining diners sat speechless.

Look after her? Ruthia thought.

After breakfast, Livia opened the doors to Hiram's study where she found him standing at the window. He turned to her.

"Livy."

"I need to speak with you, Hiram."

"What is it?"

"I am going a way for a while with the twins."

"Where?"

Where—that is all that matters? What about why? "To visit Kade."

"Aye," he said, looking out the window.

She waited anxiously for him to object or offer to accompany them, but he did not.

"How long will you be gone?" he asked, seemingly unconcerned.

She was unprepared for this question; she never thought the conversation would progress to this. His obvious apathetic attitude initiated the only proper response in her opinion.

"Indefinitely."

She turned and left. She was wiping the tears from her cheeks when Rahzvon met her in the hall. He gently caught her by the arm.

"Livia, what's he done, now?"

"Nothing—absolutely nothing! I am leaving and he could not care less! He thinks only of *her!*" She fled for the stairs.

Rahzvon stood motionless. Life was repeating itself. How many times over the years had he reprimanded Hiram for his unconscionable behavior? All those memories culminated into one raging fury. He stormed into the study.

"Have you no brains, man?" he bellowed.

"I'm finished discussing Elizabeth with you, Mr. Sierzik!"

"No you're not!" He slammed the doors into their pockets and then went face-to-face with Hiram.

"I neither know how you feel about Miss Clayton, nor do I care, but I *do* care how little *you* care for your *wife!* I've warned you too many times in the past—I'm finished warning you! I'm sick to death of being your advisor for a marriage you do not deserve!"

"How dare you—" Hiram snarled.

"Quite easily! Your wife is leaving, Hiram! Do you know why?" he scorned.

"To see Kade and—"

"No! Are you *blind*? She left crying because of *your* ridiculous jealousy over my son and his feelings for Miss Clayton, who is not one-tenth the woman that Livia is—mother of Kade and your twins! You dare take the chance of losing one of the most wonderful women on this earth—over some silly notion that you should rekindle a relationship of years passed? You're a fool and you had better grow up before your life is a lonely shambles with NO family!"

Sophia had watched Rahzvon enter Hiram's study and she had remained in the hall, witnessing her husband's fury. She felt a deep sadness for all involved: Livia, her uncle and her husband. She felt sympathy for Livia and although she loved her uncle, he was making a foolish error in judgment. As for her husband, she felt pure pride at his attempt to confront her uncle. However, none of this should have happened. Why did it have to be such a small world? Why did Von's teacher have to be Hiram's former sweetheart?

Rahzvon stopped on his way out. "Talk to him, Phia." Then he stormed away.

Sophia slowly entered the study and closed the door. Hiram was sitting behind his desk and staring at the floor.

"Uncle Hiram?"

"Sophia, you needn't say a word. Rahzvon was right. He brought it so *subtly* to my attention. I have been behaving like a lad, no older than Von."

"We've all made mistakes. Even I probably have."

This understatement brought a smile to his face. "Come here, Sophia." He put his arms around her and embraced her. "You have brought so much to my life since you first arrived. You were barely Von's age."

"You mean giving you the triplets and Ivy."

"Not only the children, but the unexpected joy that you and that cantankerous husband have given me and the clan. I admit that he has pulled me out of more than one sticky wicket."

"He is a marvel." She looked up at him in search of his humble side. "So is Livia."

"Aye. She is my life. Call all of this temporary insanity."

"It will be permanent, if you don't make amends with Livia, *now*."

"You're right." He hugged her again and left.

One relationship solved, but there is still Von's dilemma, she thought. That issue would have to be addressed at a later date, as Von and Liza left for London the next day. Livia and the twins did not. After a long heart-to-heart talk and a great deal of tolerance on Livia's part, Hiram convinced her that he had been a fool and was sorely contrite for insulting her and nearly destroying their cherished marriage.

***

Later that week, Zanya was sitting in the garden, working on her latest manuscript when Rufus sat down beside her.

"Mornin', *Wee One.*"

She laughed, "*Wee* One? Where did you hear that? That's what my father calls me—well not exactly, 'Littlest One.' And *where* did you come from?"

"Down the road and I just made up the name."

"Great men think alike, I guess. How have you been?"

"Bored."

"Not happy as a landlubber?"

He shrugged.

"What about your plans for the fishing fleet?"

He stared at the table. "Temporarily on hold."

She lifted the pitcher and filled the empty glass in front of her. "Here, it's clean—I haven't used it."

"What is it?"

"Grape Kool-Aid—it just came in at the mercantile."

He took it and drank half. "Tasty. I wouldna cared if ye had."

"Had what?"

"Drank from it."

"Oh...Why the long face? Are you still upset about...Jeanie."

"Nay, 'tis water under the bridge."

"Well you're down in the mouth about something? Care to discuss it? I've had ample practice as a good listener with Ruthia and Ivy as sisters."

"Will ye walk wit' me? I think better on me feet."

"Sure. Let me finish this one thought." She scribbled for a minute and then placed a large rock on the pages of her manuscript. "That ought to hold them." She took the arm he offered her.

"I hear we hae a new visitor to our fair village," he began.

"Miss Clayton? Yes. But she returned to Town with Von."

"Nay, I am 180lanning180' to that bloke Seton."

"*Bloke*? That's pretty harsh. You don't like him?"

"Ruthia is spendin' a lot o' time wit' him."

"Yes, how did you know that?"

"Grandma Dugan may be brightenin' London wit' her gossip, but word still gets around."

"The rumors are correct. Ruthia thinks that Stanford Seton is her knight in shining armor." She rolled her eyes.

"Why is he here?"

"He came to visit Marvin and is setting up a base for his business, here."

"He's stayin' permanently?"

"That's what Ruthia says."

"I met him at the pub. Nay, I dunna trust him. There's somethin' shifty 'bout him," he said, shaking his head.

She stopped at the fountain. "Give me a boost up, please." He held her waist and lifted her up onto the fountain wall. "Mr. McTavish, do I sense a hint of jealousy? Are you sure that your dislike for Mr. Seton is not misguided by your interest in my sister?"

He stopped and stared at her. "Verra perceptive, *Wee One.*"

"Hardly, you're not the first to have a crush on the Sierzik social butterfly...You know, it just so happens that Mr. Seton has left for a while on a fishing trip with Marvin."

"Aye?" He leaned back against the wall. "Do ye think that she might dine wit' me and me family in Langford?"

"You can ask. There is no harm in that. She could surprise you. I know that she has always had a special place in her heart for you, fickle that she is."

"Do ye think that I should?"

"No guarantees what will come of it, but you'll never know until you ask."

"I am goin' to. Right now! Is she in?"

"Yes. Go ask Miles to announce you."

"I will!" He started running towards the backdoor.

"Hey, come get me down, first!"

He stopped, and ran back.

"Sorry, *Wee One*." He lifted her down.

"Thank you, and Rufus use the front door. It will make a better impression."

He nodded, smiled and took off.

Miles announced Rufus, and Ruthia greeted him with sincere delight, as her social calendar was temporarily blank.

"Hello, Rufus! How wonderful to see you! Come sit next to me on the divan in the parlor."

"Ruthia." He nodded shyly and followed her in.

She looked at him inquisitively. Something was different about him. "I haven't seen you since the party."

He glanced around the room. "Me and me pa hae been travellin' back and forth to Town, tryin' to get Grandma settled in. Right when we think she has everythin', she thinks o'182nothin' else."

"I see...Lochmoor Glen seems like a ghost town, since she and Mrs. Zigmann moved away."

"Aye, but the two are as happy as two peas in a pod. She wasna there five minutes before they were planning' their outin's." He glanced to the ceiling.

"That's wonderful. I'm planning to do a bit of travelling, myself," she said with a grin.

"Aye, where?" he asked apprehensively.

"To the Paris fashion show," she boasted.

"Alone?" He sat up.

"Of course not, Mr. Stanford Seton will be escorting me."

"Alone?" he repeated indignantly.

"Von and his mentor will be joining us," she said with an air of sophistication.

"Why would *Seton* want to go to a fashion show? Is he a dress designer, too?" he snickered.

She turned to him. "No, silly. He is going because *I* am going."

"He seems to hae a lot o' free time."

"He's an entrepreneur; his time is governed by him alone," she said with pride.

"What is his business?"

"He imports and sells gadgets of sorts. He has to travel extensively. He is quite worldly."

"Is he out bein' worldly, now?"

"No, just fishing in Eyemouth with Marvin."

"For how long?"

"A week or so, I am sorry to say." She sighed.

"I am not."

"What do you mean by that comment, Mr. McTavish?"

"Ruthia, will ye join me and me family for supper in Langford?"

"At the inn? I would love to go. I haven't visited with Mercy in ages! What time?"

"Uh... I suppose we will pick ye up 'bout seven."

"Perfect!" She gave him a peck on the cheek. "I have to decide what to wear! See you tonight!"

Rufus remained in the parlor rehashing the conversation. Ruthia's interest in his mother had caught him off guard.

"Did you ask her?" Zanya asked from the doorway.

"Aye."

She walked over to him. "Did she accept?"

"Aye."

She sat down next to him. "You don't seem too happy about it."

He leaned back into the divan. "'Tis goin' to be more difficult than I thought."

She got up and put her hands on her hips. "It's every man for himself, Rufus McTavish, and you have an entire week to win her over."

He slapped his thighs and stood up.

"Yer right, *Wee One*. Thank ye!"

"You are welcome, Rufus."

Chapter 12

"Home, Sweet Home"

"Love can make any place agreeable."

—American proverb

From that moment on, Rufus jumped at every opportunity to "win Ruthia over."

His agenda included a day of fishing at the Brachney Hall pond, a horseback ride up to Duncan Ridge, and a picnic in the woods between the McDonnally estates. All appeared to be going well. As Ruthia seemed to be truly enjoying his company, Rufus's confidence in the relationship was at an all-time high.

On the fourth day, they spent the evening with Phemie while Tavy and Mercy went to supper. Rufus felt this experience might be conducive to introducing parenting to he and Ruthia. They were having a good time until Rufus made the fatal mistake of one little comment: "Just think, one day there may be a Phia and Phemia in the same family!" This cost him the remainder of that evening and the final days of the week—Ruthia instantly withdrew from the relationship.

At last, the day arrived; Stan had returned. Ruthia spent three hours preparing for his visit. This involved beauty face treatments, a manicure, wardrobe planning and brief conversations with her reflection to check her expressions for the right impression.

That evening, he called on her. Zanya inadvertently witnessed the romantic union in the front hall. She then realized that her friend Rufus's chances to win over her sister were slim to none. That very hour Ruthia came rushing into Zanya's room.

"Zonnie, it's happening!"

"What?"

"He wants to dine with me alone. He says he has something of great importance to discuss with me!"

"He probably wants to consult with you about what color of yo-yo will sell better," Zanya giggled.

"Funny. He is going to propose—I can feel it!" She placed her hand on her heart.

"You had better feel it quietly, before Mother and Father hear."

"You're right—this has to be handled properly...now, I have to find the perfect outfit!"

Once Ruthia left, Zanya put down her pencil and pad. *Von gone, and maybe Ruthie, too?* "It's sure going to be quiet around here."

Stan picked up Ruthia that evening and drove her to the Strickland residence There they shared an intimate meal, as Jeanie and Marvin were out dining with Martha Wheaton and Conrad. The seven-course meal was delectable, the conversation strained. Small talk reigned. Being incredibly nervous in anticipation of the upcoming discussion, Ruthia offered very few comments. The afters were being served when Stanford reached for her hand—the first promising sign.

"Ruthia, while I was away, relaxing, I had

a great deal of time to contemplate my future. We've not known each other for very long, but our time together has forced me to reassess my goals. My plans to be a travelling entrepreneur and investor were once my only desire. But having been away from you for only one week—I felt an incredible void form in my life."

"You did?" she asked meekly.

"Yes, a void that I never want to experience, again." He pulled a velvet box from his vest pocket and opened it. "Miss Ruthia Sierzik, will you do me the honor of being Mrs. Seton?"

She stared at the ring. It was beautiful—larger and more extravagant than any she had seen. This was too good to be true. Was she dreaming? But, was Stanford all that she wanted in a husband? He had brought a new light into her life. Her parents would have new respect for her. They would think of her as a responsible adult. She saw success in a union with this man.

"Ruthia?"

She pulled her gaze away from the ring to his adoring eyes. "Yes, my darling. Yes!"

He removed the ring, placed it on her finger, and sealed the engagement with a kiss.

"I love you Stanford Seton."

"I know." He smiled and hugged her.

Ruthia did not waste any time in

announcing her exciting news. Her father voiced his objection, as Mr. Seton had not solicited his approval for his daughter's hand, denying him any opportunity to refuse him. As for Sophia, she assured her husband that times were changing and that courtesy was no longer necessary, although she secretly believed it was.

In a few weeks, Stanford would accompany Ruthia, Zanya and Martha to join Von and Liza in London. The four would then fly to Paris together for the fashion show while Zanya and Martha visited with Harriet and Eloise. Prior to that, Mr. Seton was full of surprises—one of which Ruthia had not anticipated.

One afternoon, a few days before the trip, Stanford picked up Ruthia from the McDonnally Mansion for a mysterious drive. So mysterious, in fact, that he insisted that Ruthia wear a blindfold. When they arrived at their destination, he removed it.

Her face numb, Ruthia asked, "What are we doing here?"

"This, future Mrs. Seton, is your surprise engagement gift—our new home!"

"You're playing a joke on me," she said fearfully.

"No, I am quite serious. Surprised?" He got out of the car, opened her door, and helped her out. "I made the transaction this morning."

"Transaction?"

"Paid in full, darling."

He led her to the front door.

She looked towards the heavens. *Please, Lord, no.* This was no mansion or a gorgeous home like that of the Stricklands. This was unbelievable.

"Wait until you see inside. It's so quaint, Ruthia."

"Stan, I don't need to see inside."

"Dearest, look at it—it's a piece of art—turned like that. They say it survived a twister! Don't you just love it?"

Her expression was noncommittal. "This is the house that I grew up in," she muttered.

"You're pulling my leg?" He took a step back and put his hands on his hips.

"No, Stan."

"Hm? What an...ironic coincidence...well, darling, welcome back," he said feebly and unlocked the door.

Ruthia stepped inside. It was just as her family had left it years ago.

"Fond memories?" he asked cautiously.

She was at a crossroads. She could either tell the man whom she loved that she abhorred the idea of living in her childhood home and risk hurting his feelings...or she could pretend that it was her dream come true—to live out her life in this old, small house and in the process, stay in his good graces. The latter was not preferable, but there was the future to consider—a move to a larger estate, if she played her cards right. Even Jeanie had refused to live in that magnificent, family estate and had convinced Marvin to surprise her with a new home.

"How thoughtful, Stan." She forced a smile.

"I confess—I can't take credit. I had no idea that it was your family's residence."

"How fateful," she mumbled.

She followed him through the rooms. His favorite was her father's little library upstairs.

"What are all those?" She pointed at the crates and barrels lining the walls.

"My merchandise. I prefer to uses this as my office, in the future, but now it doubles as a miniature warehouse."

"I see."

After the painfully nostalgic tour, Ruthia was a woman of few words on the return to the manor. Her shock and discomfort escalated when Stan mentioned that she was only a short distance from her family—an added benefit? She would have someone with whom to visit when he was gone, travelling for *weeks* at a time. As they approached the manor, she silently rehearsed the role of the adoring bride-to-be—overwhelmed and thrilled with the prospect of taking up housekeeping in her *very* unexpected engagement gift.

Her performance convinced the majority of the clan that she was pleased with the arrangement. However, Zanya suspected otherwise. That evening, Zanya confronted her.

"Ruthie, why would you agree to this? You hate our old house. We have had countless discussions about leaving there, and, besides, you've always wanted a larger home."

Ruthia closed the wardrobe doors and turned to her sister with tear-filled eyes.

"Zonnie, what choice did I have?"

She took Ruthia's hands in hers. "He's to be your husband. You need to be honest with him."

"I know, but he was so excited about it. He took me their blindfolded to surprise me."

"Well, he definitely succeeded in that. Do you think that you can actually live there for *years* and be truly happy? It is one thing to live in a smaller house—but *that* one?"

"I love him Zonnie. I suppose I can tolerate it for a short while." She collapsed to the bed.

"Ruthie, what if you never get the chance to move and have to raise a family there?"

"Don't even say it!" She slapped the mattress.

"Then perhaps, you need to discuss this with him. He loves you—he should understand. Otherwise, it will be a point of contention between the two of you. I'm no expert, but it doesn't seem to be a good way to start out a marriage."

Ruthia fell back on the bed. "I'll talk to him...after we return from Paris."

She stared at the canopy above her. Living

in *that* house was not the only thing troubling her. The fact that Stan was planning to be gone for weeks at a time was another issue. If he loved her and missed her so much, why would he leave her at *that* house? Why didn't he ask her to travel with him? She had no responsibilities to tie her down. *Did* he truly love her? He had never once said so. Would he understand about the house? Oh, how she wished that she could share these doubts with her sister. But, she dare not admit to making a wrong decision, again.

Taking Ruthia's hand and pulling her up to sit, Zanya insisted, "Don't let it spoil your trip. Cheer up. Let's go down and test those juicy blackberry scones, I smell baking."

The next day, Zanya was visiting Smitty at Brachney Hall. After discussing Smitty's break up with Kade for a good hour, the two headed downstairs in search of a snack. There they met Rufus handing the cook a string of fish; she took them with a grateful smile.

"Mornin', Zanya, Smitty." He gestured with his free hand

"You're just the man I wanted to see," Smitty said.

She took a hold of Zanya's arm with her free hand. "Be an angel and entertain Miss Sierzik for a half hour."

"Alright, but I warn ye, me halo is a bit tarnished."

"That's Zanya's problem, not mine!" Smitty giggled. "Got to run—I forgot to practice and my piano teacher will be here, tonight. Mother will be furious if she hears one more complaint from her. Thanks, Rufus. I'd better shake a leg. See you two later."

"Shall we *fly* down to the pond? It is such a beautiful day," Zanya laughed.

"Me pleasure, *Wee One*," he said, taking her hand, leading her to the pond.

They sat down on the bank after skipping a few stones.

"The week wit' Ruthia didna go too well."

"I heard. I'm sorry."

"Do ye think I might get anot'er chance?"

"Rufus...Ruthia is engaged, now." She looked at him sympathetically.

"Nay...so soon?" His eyes pleaded.

"Yes. He proposed the day that he returned from the fishing trip."

Rufus dropped his head in defeat.

"Don't feel so badly. Ruthia's not the only available girl in Lochmoor Glen."

He shrugged.

"What about Dara Wheaton. She speaks very highly of you."

"She's a fine lassie, but predictable. Not like Ruthia. There's no one here for me. Maybe I should move on. I canna bear to see Ruthia wit' him—'twas enough seein' Jeanie wit' Strickland."

"But where would you go?" she said with concern.

"Out to sea," he said solemnly, looking out across the pond.

"*Rufus McTavish,*" her voice demanded that he look at her. "Shame on you—you can't just leave your home because a relationship doesn't work out. If the dear Lord has someone for you, you will meet her when He is ready. You needn't run away from friends and family, in the meantime. A handsome man like you won't go unnoticed for long...That beautiful head of hair will draw attention wherever you go."

"Aye, like a red beacon in the night, ye canna miss it." He shook his head.

"Do you have any idea how many women would cherish the opportunity to be seen in your company? You're so tall and strong and your facial features are so..." she said, seemingly lost in studying them. She caught herself, "And you're so kind and fun!" She leaned back in the grass.

He sat motionless. She was so sweet, so gentle. The tiny Zanya with a big heart.

She sat up. "Rufus, on second thought, Ruthia and Seton may be engaged, but they're not married. Their relationship is not finalized—set in stone, as yet."

He faced her. "What would ye be insinuatin'?"

"I have an idea; do you have any plans for

the fourteenth?"

"Nay."

"How would you like to visit your grandmother?"

That evening, Zanya informed her family of the change in plans.

"Mother, Father, Ruthia, I've invited Rufus, instead of Martha, to join us on the trip to London."

Ruthia squinted with suspicion. "Rufus? Why?"

"Because he, too, is going to London to visit Mrs. Dugan. It's silly for Rufus to travel the same route, alone. Economically, it'll save on petrol."

Rahzvon intervened from behind his copy of the newspaper. "Good. I prefer it. I like the idea of another man going along."

"Why's that, Father?" Ruthia demanded.

He dropped the paper. "Don't use that tone with me. The truth is that I'm not sold on Seton, yet. I trust Rufus."

"Father, he's my fiancé! Rufus is a sailor!"

Rahzvon thought back. Years ago, the honorable little Rufus had run his legs off helping him with his postal route. "I trust Rufus—I know him."

Sophia closed her magazine and jumped to Ruthia's defense. "In time, Rahzie, I'm sure that you will get to know Sten...as well as you do your own son."

"Good example, Phia. After seventeen years I knew Von so well—my son the dress designer, head over heels for a woman who's too old for me." He began reading again.

"I should say so, Mr. Sierzik! And don't you forget it!" Sophia exclaimed and then looked at the shocked faces of her two oldest daughters. She dropped her mending in the basket. "Ruthia, not to worry, he'll come to love Stenford."

"*Stanford* Mother."

"Yes, dear, goodnight. Good night, Zanya. Coming, dear?" Sophia asked bluntly.

Rahzvon threw his paper onto the divan and followed her out.

The trip to London went as planned. While Zanya sat in the backseat enjoying Rufus's hilarious fishing stories, Ruthia sat up front— a prisoner of Stan's recitation of humdrum facts and figures regarding wholesale marketing. More often than not, Ruthia tuned out her fiancé's commentary, to listen to the sailor's exciting escapades. By the time they reached London, Ruthia began to question a future with the self-absorbed capitalist.

When the four parted ways, Ruthia watched enviously as her sister strolled away, giggling with her entertaining escort. However, Ruthia, like her mother, was a survivor and optimized her concentration on the upcoming fashion show.

***

Ruthia and Stan met Von and Miss Clayton in front of the hotel. After the Sierzik siblings' somewhat awkward embrace, Ruthia introduced Stan.

"Miss Clayton, Von, this is my fiancé, Stanford Seton. Stan—my brother Von and his art instructor, Miss Clayton."

Stan glanced at Von's outstretched hand then shook it, while admiring the sweet smile of Von's date. He then addressed her.

"Miss Clayton, this is a great pleasure. You have made a renowned mark on the fashion industry."

"I thank you. Familiar with fashion design, Mr. Seton?"

"Most certainly. I follow it closely."

Ruthia took hold of his arm, "You never mentioned that to me," she said pointedly.

"Ruthia, you never mentioned your *engagement*," Von said tersely.

"Congratulations to both of you," Miss Clayton quickly redirected the conflict. "Shall we catch our flight?"

Chapter 13

"Parisian Style"

"You can fool all of the people some of the time and you can fool some of the people all of the time, but you can't fool all of the people all of the time."

—Abraham Lincoln

The four took a cab to the airport and boarded the Imperial Airways plane from London to Paris.

Stan made a point of strategically taking the seat next to Miss Clayton, with Von on her right. Ruthia sat in the seat across the aisle from Stan. To her dismay, not only did a large man smoking a putrid cigar sit on her left, but for the duration of the trip, Stan conversed *only* with Miss Clayton. On occasion, he would look over at Ruthia and throw her a verbal tidbit like, "Doing okay, honey?" or "Need something to drink or eat, sweetheart?" Von also appeared to be irritated with his future brother-in-law. Von glanced repeatedly from his magazine to the window, trying to ignore the dialogue between Seton and Liza. Ruthia could feel her once undisputable physical, emotional and mental attraction for Mr. Know It All Seton—dwindling away. What was she doing with *this* arrogant, fickle man who nearly avoided eye contact with her since that first moment when he met Miss Clayton? The fashion show was quickly losing its appeal.

Arrogant as Stanford appeared to be, he was no fool. That evening he arrived at Ruthia's door.

"My future Mrs. Seton, you look breathtaking! The runway models will die of envy when they see you," he remarked when Ruthia, wearing Chinese red lipstick and a fur-trimmed evening gown opened the door to the Ritz Hotel room that she shared with Miss Clayton. She modestly thanked him, but then held her breath. What compliment would he have for Miss Clayton, wrapped up like a Christmas present in her own hand-painted silk, creation?

Ruthia's confidence was instantly restored when he greeted Liza, "Good evening, Miss Clayton. Lovely."

The three continued, to pick up Von at his room. He had conveniently declined Stanford's invitation to share a room with him, claiming that he wanted to spare Stan the displeasure of his snoring. Ruthia knew otherwise; Von did not snore.

After a great deal of effort to make their way through the congested Paris streets, the couples arrived at the coveted fashion show. Fortunately, for Ruthia and Von's sake, the couples were not seated together. Von was delighted to have Liza all to himself and Ruthia considered it to be nothing less than an act of God to have Miss Clayton out of earshot.

Ruthia's dream to view the industry's presentations was just as she had imagined it would be. She enjoyed every second of the show. If only she could afford a wardrobe of those new designs. It was bittersweet—purely window-shopping with no funds. However, there was some consolation in that this problem may vanish if she became Mrs. Seton.

It was not until the last of the models made her debut donning one particular outfit that caught the attention of the two couples, simultaneously. The tall woman wearing tight blond waves pressed close to her head, started down the runway.

Stan leaned over toward Ruthia. "There it is, darling!"

"What about it?"

"That's mine," he said proudly.

She glared at the model, then him. "Your what?" she asked suspiciously.

"My design!"

"What?"

"I own it. It is one of my investments."

"Darling...I'm impressed." She touched his hand.

"Dear, you would be surprised at the avenues that my capital takes."

"I *am*." She studied the beautiful design. "It is stunning!"

"Yes, it is." He nodded proudly.

Several aisles away, Von slipped into a dazed state. He focused on the model whose stride was slowing down as an approaching phantom in the midst of the crowd's muffled oohs and ah's. He could not believe it—his choked whisper barely escaped his lips.

"That is my design. I created it." His breathing quickened.

"Von, what do you mean?" Liza asked,

confused.

"That is my design! I created it!" he repeated through clenched teeth.

"Sh!" a bald man with thick glasses and a goatee warned, as he tapped on Von's shoulder.

"Von, are you sure. It probably just resembles one that—" Liza whispered.

"No—that is mine—the backless dress, 'V' neckline with ruffles, deep scarlet rayon, tight at the hips and waist—the flower on the shoulder and on the hip! Even the shoe-shaped hat and matching handbag are all mine!"

"Will you please be quiet!" the man behind them demanded.

"But how could this be, Von?" Liza whispered.

"I will tell you how—that is #14 in my sketchbook—which was stolen!" he whispered fiercely.

"Stolen from my studio?"

"No—from my room at home!" He tightened his grip on the arms of the seat.

"Not here, Von. Calm down. Why don't you go outside? I will tell Ruthia that you are not feeling well." She tugged on his arm.

"You bet I'm not," he snarled.

"I'll meet you outside," she whispered as he pushed his way through annoyed audience.

After the show, Ruthia, unaware of Von's

anger about the presentation, said good night to Stanford and went directly to Von's room. She knocked at the door.

"Vonnie, let me in, please, I want to talk to you."

He jerked open the door glaring at her— the sister who had *lost* his sketchbook!

"How ill are you?" she asked with concern.

"Sick to death!" He threw up his arms. "What do you think?" he shouted.

"I understand, Von, but she really is too old for you. It is better that she told you, now."

"What?" he asked fiercely.

"You and Miss Clayton—it's no secret that Mother and Father are worried to death about you."

Von was angry with Ruthia *before* she arrived, but now his livid words could not be expelled quickly enough.

"Out Ruthia! Out! Go home! This is *all* your fault!"

"But Von—"

He took her arm and quickly escorted her to the hall, slammed the door, and locked it. However, Ruthia did not let his response upset her. She was sympathetic and understood. His relationship with Miss Clayton would not be easily dismissed. She thought back to how he had doted over his instructor when he had brought her to meet the family.

Ruthia returned to her room. Elizabeth was asleep. It was for the best; Ruthia had a nagging desire to offer a few unsavory words for the woman who had lured her brother into an inappropriate relationship and then jilted him.

The flight back to London was awkward at best. Ruthia observed Von and Elizabeth. They conversed very little. Stanford, too, kept to himself, busy figuring in a small black notebook.

When they arrived in London, Von and Ruthia shared only a farewell nod. Ruthia faked a smile for Miss Clayton, and took Stan's arm to walk to the Zigmann/Dugan cottage. After a short visit, the original foursome, Ruthia, Stan, Zanya, and Rufus were reunited for the journey back to Lochmoor Glen.

At the onset of the trip, Zanya said sadly, "I really missed seeing Von."

"Zonnie, you can be glad that you didn't. He was in quite an evil mood," Ruthia remarked.

"I wish you wouldn't use that slang."

"Okay, he was feeling incredibly low. I'll explain later."

"Well, now, how was the show?" Zanya asked, with genuine enthusiasm.

"Fantastic! You won't *believe* whose design made a superb hit."

"Whose?"

"My future husband's!"

"Stan's?" she asked, bowled over.

He spoke up. "As I explained to my sweetheart, *mine* as an investment."

"That explains *your* desire to attend the show," Zanya surmised.

"Just another surprise for my little woman—you heard about the house?"

Zanya glanced nervously at Rufus. She had forewarned him of the engagement, but had not mentioned the gift Stan had given his future bride.

"House?" Rufus asked.

"Yes, a lovely little home. Was *she* ever surprised," Stan reported.

"Yes, she was," Zanya confirmed.

Ruthia remained silent. Could she tell Stan that she was displeased with the house when they returned home? She glanced over at him while he rattled on about sales curves and spewed out percentages. In her frustration, she made a quick attempt to avoid any further monologues.

"Now tell me about your visit in London, Zonnie."

"It was simply glorious! We went to the movies and the dance clubs and had a wonderful time playing gin with Mrs. Dugan and Eloise." She sighed. "We sure packed a lot into a short time, didn't we Rufus?"

"Aye, what did we get—maybe three hours of sleep last night?"

"Two and a half." Zanya yawned.

"Rufus, why not tell us some more of your

sea stories," Ruthia asked eagerly.

"Nay, I think I will be nappin' a bit." He slid down in his seat.

Ruthia leaned back, thoroughly disappointed. She was nearly bored to tears while Stan recounted his marketing issues with garbage disposals. Zanya rested peacefully with her head on Rufus's shoulder.

Phemie was euphoric at the couples' return to Lochmoor Glen. She was thrilled to see her brother Rufus and quickly forgave him for not taking her to visit Grandma Dugan when he presented one of Grandpa's twiglets to her. Life in the village continued as usual.

That following week, Zanya agreed to help Ruthia redecorate her new "old" house.

"Are you sure that you want to go through with this, Ruthie?"

"Zanya, I told you that I changed my mind. I can't bear to hurt Stan's feelings."

"Hurt is feelings? He wasn't too concerned about yours—up and running out on you for two weeks."

"It is necessary. His work demands it. I am not like Jeanie Wheaton—I mean Strickland. I like my time alone...occasionally."

"More often than not?" Zanya raised a brow.

"I don't care to discuss it. Come on—let's get creative. I want an entirely different house when we're finished." She headed upstairs with her sister following.

"What are you going to do with Dad's library?" Zanya asked.

"I suppose Stan has his own decorating ideas," Ruthia said, peeking in through the doorway.

"It looks as though he's already started." Zanya pointed to the frame on the adjacent wall.

"Oh, that's it—his design investment! Come see!"

The two weaved through the crates and barrels.

"Yes, Zonnie, that is it. To think that I actually saw it modeled in real life." Ruthia sighed.

Zanya took a step closer. "Great Scott, that's Von sketch from his sketch book!"

"It is not!"

"It is! Look here in the corner—the initials VS."

"It can't be."

"Look at the page size, Ruthia. It's from Von's sketchbook."

Ruthia stood, staring blankly.

"Von saw *his* design modeled at the Paris show?" Zanya asked, flabbergasted.

She nodded and sat down on a barrel.

"How did he react when he saw it?" Zanya demanded.

"I don't know...We weren't seated

together."

"Poor, poor Vonnie, he must have been devastated. Ruthia, do you know what this means?"

Ruthia looked up fearfully.

"Your fiancé stole our brother's sketch and sold it without his approval!"

"He didn't know it was Von's. I'm sure of it. If he knew it was his, he wouldn't have dared witness Von seeing it at the show, let alone post it in our house for all to see."

"Perhaps not, but the fact that it is in his possession, remains the same. If he has one, he has them all!"

"Well, I'll just get them back."

"How? Do you have a clue where his sketchbook is? He obviously got it from Marvin's home."

"It has to be here, somewhere." She scanned the tiny room.

"Then you had better search every crate and barrel until you find it or the clan will tar and feather you alongside your thieving fiancé! Goodbye, Ruthia."

Ruthia ran after her. "Wait, Zanya, what about the decorating!"

"Forget it, I've seen enough!"

Zanya left without turning back. Ruthia sat glumly in the sea of inventory. "I think that I've seen enough, too."

Opening and searching all of the containers was one incredible task, but returning all to its original state was quite another. *What have I done? Why did I ever touch that blasted sketchpad?* Time was the only thing on her side; Stan would be gone for two weeks. She let out a sigh and began the dreaded search.

Still reeling from the dire situation, Zanya stormed into the McDonnally mansion. She was speaking aloud to herself, not noticing that her great uncle Hiram had stepped out of his study to check on all the commotion.

Zanya ranted, as she entered the staircase, "That Ruthia beats all! This is the last straw! I feel no sympathy for her. She is tainting the very soul of our childhood home with her shenanigans!"

Hiram called out to her, "Disagreement about the decorating?" he asked, grinning.

"I could only wish it was something as insignificant as that. This is serious!" She started toward the staircase.

"What has she done?"

"It's not my place to say!" She marched up the stairs.

Having had a special place in his heart for Ruthia since the day she was born, Hiram could not bear to think that she had gotten herself into more trouble. She, like he, was a misunderstood individual.

"Miles!" he summoned.

"Sir?"

"Please, tell Mrs. McDonnally that I shall return within the hour. I am going to pay Ruthia a visit at her house."

"I will tell her, directly, sir."

"Thank you, Miles."

Hiram drove up to the future home of Mr. and Mrs. Seton. He knocked, but no one answered. He opened the door.

"Ruthia?" he called.

"Uncle Hiram. I'm up here!" She leaned out into the hall.

She tossed a cover over the grate of tape dispensers and rushed to the hall.

"Since I was in the area, I thought I would see how the renovations are progressing."

"It is quite a bit to tackle, especially since Zanya left. She's helping me to create a new look for my new life," she said, glancing nervously toward the library.

His gaze followed hers. "Already moving in, I see."

"Not me. Those are Stan's things—his merchandise." She put her hands on her hips and surveyed the area.

"Aye. I understand that he has quite a broad array of investments."

"What?" her voice cracked.

"All kinds of gadgets."

"Yes, yes, all kinds." She gestured and explained, "All these contain different little inventions. It is quite fascinating."

"Are these his samples?"

"No, this is everything—his inventory."

"All of it?" He tilted his head.

"Yes. He wants to use this for an office, once he is established."

"Ruthia, I must say that I cannot imagine any man able to support a wife, selling so little."

"There's actually quite a lot in each crate." She removed the cover, took out a little tape dispenser from the crate, and handed it to him.

"What's this?"

"Cellophane tape in a dispenser—it's like a sticky glued strip to hold paper together."

"Hmm?" He turned it over in his hand.

"And you can see through it."

"I could have used this when a document was torn, yesterday."

"It's yours, with Stan's compliments. He wouldn't mind," she said smiling. "Anything to get the word out."

Hiram took it and placed it in his coat pocket. "Thank you."

She caught a peripheral glimpse of the framed sketch and took his arm to remove him to the hall.

"Have some tea with me, Uncle Hiram?"

"With my dear lassie? Of course."

After a casual chat over tea, Hiram, still unaware of the origin of Zanya's fury, returned to his estate.

He went directly to his study to experiment with his cellophane tape. "Hmm?" He removed it from his pocket and tore off the cellophane wrapper.

"Interesting." He examined it, turning it upside down. A small piece of brown butcher's paper was wedged between the metal sides. He pulled it out.

"Packing?" He tossed it onto the desk and pulled the starter strip.

"Voille! Look at that," he said, holding a foot of outstretched tape.

"Amazing." He carefully wound it back on the roll with as much dexterity as his large fingers would permit.

"Where's that form?" He rummaged through his files in the second drawer on the right.

"Aha!" He laid the torn paper on the desktop and smoothed the "S" tear—the result from a hand in a fit of anger over the acceptance of an *unacceptable,* but necessary bid. He placed the newly pulled strip so it straddled the tear and then pressed it down—then, a second strip to complete the repair. "Grand!" I have to hand it to Seton—a wise investment."

He pulled an envelope from the third drawer, folded the bid and placed it inside. He lifted the paperweight and placed the envelope under it, after depositing his newly acquired dispenser in the top drawer.

He snatched the folded packing to toss it in the dustbin when he stopped. "What's this?" The little folded piece of slightly bulging, thin, brown paper was taped together on one end. He carefully caught his nail under the edge of the tape and peeled it off. No longer restrained, the packet slowly opened on its own.

Hiram stared at the contents: fine and white, like talc or confectioner's sugar—innocent looking enough, perhaps when found among the toiletries or sundries of four o'clock tea, but not here. The white powder filled the sharp folds of the packet, leaving chalky dustings along the broader surfaces.

He could not bring himself to touch it—in his mind that would somehow confirm its fantastic incongruous presence in his study—making its arrival in the safe little world he had so carefully built for his family more...definite—*real*. So, it sat—a repulsive presence on the shiny surface of his desk, its snow-white purity infinitely more malevolent than the, polished obsidian gleam of a firearm or the silver edge of a knife.

So, this was how Mr. Seton could make a living on so little inventory. Did Ruthia know what her fiancé was actually peddling?

With cold fingertips, Hiram forced himself to carefully return the packet to its original configuration. He used the dispenser to tear off a small piece of tape and seal the edges back together. He took the packet and placed it in the bottom of a drawer, under a stack of proposal forms. Then he leaned back in his chair and stared at the tape dispenser in his hand.

Had this been Ruthia's subtle way of asking for his help? Why hadn't she gone to her parents? Perhaps, she still had some twisted affection for Seton and feared what would happen to him if Rahzvon discovered what he had done. Or maybe she had wanted to spare them from the ugly reality into which she had fallen.

Ruthia had said that Seton would be back in two weeks—he was probably procuring more "merchandise." Thankfully, that meant Hiram needn't attack the poor girl with questions—but they did need to extricate her from this situation as soon as possible.

"*The devil take him,*" Hiram whispered as he felt cold fury wash over him.

"Hiram?" He turned with a start. "Livy, please come in and close the doors."

"Hiram, what is it?" She moved slowly towards him, seeing something unsettling in his manner.

"Ruthia is in trouble."

"Oh no, she's not—?" Livia put her hand to her mouth.

"I certainly pray not. But this is a very serious situation."

"How serious?"

"Legal."

"She hasn't stolen, again, has she?"

"Nay—that man she is engaged to is the worst sort of filth."

"Mr. Seton?"

"Aye...and Zanya is aware of it. That is why she is upset with Ruthia. Say nothing of this to anyone."

"How could I? I have no idea of what you are speaking."

"Good. All you need to know is that Ruthia's life may be in danger and I have to speak with Zanya."

Livia stood frozen; her breathing was shallow. *Ruthia in danger?*

"Please, go Livy and ask Miles to have Zanya to report to me here."

"Yes, dear."

Chapter 14

"Life Saver"

"A narrow window may let in the light,
A tiny star dispel the gloom of night,
A little deed a mighty wrong set right."

—Florence Earle Coates

Minutes later, Zanya and Hiram were conversing privately in his study.

"Zanya, I need your help, as does your sister, Ruthia. She is in trouble."

Her eyes widened. "You know about that *rat* Seton?"

"Aye."

"She actually told you?" she asked in surprise.

"Possibly, in her own discreet way. I went to see her an hour ago."

"So you saw it?" She imagined her uncle spotting Von's sketch on the library wall.

"See it? I have it here in my drawer."

"In your drawer?" Zanya panicked. "What is she going to tell Stanford when he discovers it missing?"

"It is only one. I doubt that he will notice."

"Uncle Hiram, I know that men pay less attention to décor and detail, but it was the only thing on the library wall. And the frame is so elaborate."

"Frame, wall?" He narrowed his eyes. "Zanya, what are you talking about?"

"I thought that you knew. Von's framed sketch that Stanford stole and sold—the one modeled at the fashion show. What are *you* referring to?"

Perplexed, Hiram hesitated and then responded, "Not Von's sketch."

He pulled open the bottom drawer. He removed the packet from beneath the forms.

He held it up for her to observe.

She squinted in confusion. "What is that?"

"Seton's income—I found it tucked inside of one of his tape dispensers that Ruthia gave to me this afternoon."

She stared at the mysterious little packet. "I don't understand."

For the second time, he slowly opened it, though he was loathed to look upon it. Zanya stared in disbelief at the white powder within the paper sleeve. "What is it?" she asked slowly, her face going ashen.

He stared at her. "Probably cocaine—quite the commodity on the streets of late."

"Ruthia's fiancé is a...a drug smuggler?"

He wrapped up the evidence and returned it to the drawer. "So he has Von's sketches, too. How did *they* come into his possession?"

She let out a sigh. "You might as well know the truth. Ruthia found Von's sketchpad in his room on the night of our party. She was taking it to show our parents to alert them of his change in career. She misplaced it in the ballroom and it fell into the hands of Marvin Strickland. That is all that I know."

Hiram shook his head in disappointment. "I hope Marvin is not an accomplice to all this. Naomi and Beatrice would be devastated to discover that he is involved."

"Ruthia *is* in danger, isn't she?" Zanya choked out the inquiry.

He put his hands on her shoulders.

"Not on my watch, Zanya. I will handle this. At least, she is safe for two weeks until he returns."

As the hours passed, Ruthia continued her search for Von's sketchpad. She had just reached the final crate when she heard someone downstairs.

"Uncle Hiram, is that you?"

"No, Darling—it's me, your future husband!"

Ruthia swallowed hard. A sick feeling formed in her stomach. He had come home early. Her fingers began to tremble. She looked around frantically checking to see if everything was back in its proper place. She had found nothing—concluding that he had only the one sketch.

"I'm coming down!" She stepped into the hall.

He met her on the stairs.

"What were you doing in my office?" His brows furrowed.

"Measuring for...wallpaper and curtains. Zanya came over and was helping me."

He pushed passed her and scanned the room. The crate lid for the tape dispensers was ajar.

"Ruthia, come here," he commanded.

She slowly moved in next to him.

He grasped her arm. "You opened this crate, didn't you?" he demanded an answer.

"You're hurting me," she said, staring at him, shocked.

"Why were you going through my inventory?"

"I was curious. Please, let go of me."

He released his grip.

"You're home early," she remarked with caution.

"Change in plans." He walked briskly downstairs and turned on the final step. "I need the money that I loaned to you."

Her heart stopped and her breathing quickened. "Why?" she asked fearfully.

"That is my business. I loaned it to you in good faith and you have had weeks to repay me. I thought that I could trust you. I need it today."

"But, Stan, I don't have it."

"Get it! Someone in your almighty clan can afford to give it to you," he said sharply. He looked at his watch. "It is a quarter past five. You have until seven to bring it back here. Go, now!"

She hesitated trying to process this outrageous behavior by one who now seemed to be a stranger.

He studied her alarmed expression. His tone calmed. "Ruthia...do not mention this loan business to anyone. It is embarrassing to have to depend on your bride to rescue you from a financial scrape."

"I wouldn't think of it. After all, it was my

fault that you didn't have the four-hundred pounds."

She then moved quickly down the hall and brushed by him. She ran outside, slid behind the wheel of the McDonnally automobile and sped off.

She evaluated what had happened. He was right; she had promised to pay it back and she *had* had weeks to do so. As for Von's sketch—he may be entirely innocent in its acquirement from Marvin.

Now, for the problem at hand, whom could she ask for the cash? Although he was right, knowledge of Stan's calling in his loan would certainly color the family's opinion of him. The women would consider it inappropriate; however, the men might very well respect him for "ruling the roost."

A request at her home was not an option; Zanya and her parents would not give Stan the benefit of the doubt. She pulled into the drive at Brachney Hall. On her walk up to the house, she tried to regain her composure before rapping the doorknocker.

She knocked and Jules opened the door. "Miss Sierzik, do come in."

"Thank you, Jules. Is my Uncle Edward here?"

"Right this way. He's working on his stamp collection in the library."

Jules stopped at the doorway, "Sir, Miss Sierzik is here to see you."

Edward looked up, smiled, and left his seat. "Thank you Jules. Welcome, Ruthia, come on in and have a seat. May I offer you some refreshment?" He helped her with her chair and sat down across from her.

"No, thank you. I couldn't eat a thing."

"So, what brings you here, this evening, marriage advice?" he laughed.

"No," she said solemnly. "I'm in a pickle."

"Tell me about it, love," he said compassionately.

"It is about my engagement gift for Stan. He gave me the house, and I have nothing to give him in return."

He leaned back. "So, you need advice about what would be an appropriate gift."

"Not exactly—I've found something for him and I need to purchase it yet today or...it will be sold to another buyer."

"What is it?"

"I can't tell you. You understand; it wouldn't be proper for someone to know about it before Stan receives it."

"Ah, yes, I understand. So what is the problem?" He leaned toward her.

"I'm short of cash and I don't want to ask my parents. You know how Father is. He has certainly not kept his feelings to himself about our getting married."

"What about the gift your Aunt Naomi and I gave you?"

"Oh, I am eternally grateful, but I had to

relinquish a big part of it to Von and Zonnie as my punishment."

"This is very important to you, isn't it?"

"More than you could imagine. I mean, you only get married once...hopefully."

He pulled out his wallet. "Well, I happen to have some cash here. How much do you need?"

"*Only* four-hundred pounds."

Edward gulped. "Ruthia, is that not a bit extravagant?"

"Uncle Edward, he bought me a *house*."

"But the house is for the two of you."

"I promise that I'll pay it back. It's only a short term loan."

"All right." He nodded. "Wait here, I'll be back in a couple minutes."

Ruthia let out a sigh of relief.

He returned with the funds.

"Uncle Edward, you're a life saver! Thank you!"

"Life-Saver, eh? I guess that means that I am sweet."

"Uh...yes!" She kissed him on the cheek. "Thank you! I have to run! I'll pay you in full!"

"Darling, I'm back!" Ruthia called.

Stan stepped from the kitchen with a bottle of ale in hand.

"Well, did you get it?"

"Of course—I pay my debts."

He placed the bottle on the side table and

took her in his arms.

"Ruthia, I'm sorry for being so sharp with you. I had an unexpected snag in a contract. I misread the due date."

She let out a sigh of relief. "I understand. I have lived under my uncle Hiram's roof for some time. When a business deal goes awry, no one cares to witness his wrath."

"I promise to control my temper in the future. Now where's my welcome home?"

"Right here," she said, as she pressed her lips against his.

He then half-smiled. "And where are the banknotes?"

"Right here—all four-hundred pounds." Ruthia pulled the roll from her skirt pocket and handed it to him. "I'm sorry that it took so long."

He took her by the arm and started towards the door. "I have business to attend to and we had better get you home before it gets any later. People may begin to talk," Stan said and laughed.

"Oh, Stan," she giggled.

"Come along, I'll lock up."

She turned out the lights and snatched her cardigan. "It seems strange having electric lights here. When I was young, we had only oil lamps."

"My dear, the world is changing, every day."

He opened the car door for her. She slid

behind the wheel. He closed the door, leaned down, and kissed her. "Drive home safely. Again, I am truly sorry, my sweet. No more rages, like Hiram," he laughed.

"That's all right. He's probably quite content, now."

"And why is that?"

"I hope you don't mind, but I gave him one of your tape dispensers today."

"You did what?" Stan asked with deadly calm.

Ruthia leaned away. "Only one dispenser—I'll pay you for it." She studied his disturbing expression. "I know that I should have asked, first. I promise I will, next time."

"There won't be a next time." He opened the door. "Move over," he commanded. He slid in next to her and started the car.

"Stan, I can drive myself."

"No...I'll drive you."

"Are you angry about the dispenser?"

"No, darling, I was thinking about the contract," he said coolly.

"Oh," she said, attempting to smile.

Hiram, awaiting Ruthia's return, paced in his study. He surmised that she would not spend the night in her future home—it had no furniture. He dreaded the thought of informing her that the so-called "love of her life" was actually the lowest form of life. But, it had to be done. Hiram had arranged for Ruthia and

Zanya to leave for London, that night. Zanya had packed their clothes and necessities needed for the next three weeks. Rufus agreed to drive them to London to stay with Eloise Zigmann. When the notorious Mr. Seton would return, the authorities would be waiting for him. Tomorrow, the contraband would be safely confiscated from the old Sierzik home. The plan appeared to be foolproof.

Hiram checked the drive from his study window, no less than a half dozen times, every few minutes.

Where is she? He abandoned his post, walked to the fireplace, and leaned on the mantle. *My poor lassie, she will be devastated by the news.*

He circled his desk. Would she be so naïve as to believe that Seton was unaware of the drugs hidden in his inventory?

"I'll make her understand." He paused. *What if she refused to leave with Zanya?*

He walked back to the window. "Where are you, Ruthia?"

There was a knock on the doors.

"Come in."

"I have everything packed. Rufus is parked out back." Zanya walked to the window. "No sign of her?"

"None."

"She *was* determined to go through all the crates to find the sketchbook. It is only eight o'clock."

"Aye, did you talk to your parents?"

"I told them, just as we rehearsed: Ruthia and I are going to London to shop for her trousseau and staying with Mrs. Zigmann and we are leaving tonight, because there may be a chance of a storm, tomorrow."

"Good." He made another turn around the room. "She will not take the news, well."

"No, but she *will* thank you in the end."

Headlights flashed in the window. He ran to the hall and opened the door. "She's here," he said nervously, squinting to determine the make of the car.

Zanya rushed toward the backdoor. "I will have Rufus load the bags."

Chapter 15

"Night Ride"

"Whenever the moon and stars are set,
Whenever the wind is high,
All night long in the dark and wet,
A man goes riding by.
Late in the night when the fires are out,
Why does he gallop and gallop about?"

—Robert Louis Stevenson

Hiram stepped out into the portal where *Edward* met him.

"What brings *you* here, at this hour?" Hiram asked, surprised.

"We need to have a talk. Do you have a minute?"

"If this is about that measly bid—"

"No, it's about Ruthia."

"Come on in." Hiram quickly ushered him into his study and closed the doors. "Have you seen her?" he asked anxiously.

"Yes. I have—she payed me a visit earlier this evening. She wanted a loan."

"For what?"

"To buy her intended an engagement gift— to reciprocate for the house. I would not have said anything to you, but the circumstances left me suspicious. I know that you dote on her Hiram, but she wanted a *very* large loan."

"How large?"

"£400 and she had to have it immediately to purchase this *secret* gift because another buyer was waiting in the wings, so to speak. It was to remain a secret—the groom's privilege to see it first. You and I both are aware that there is no one in the area with anything of value for sale—not since the jewelry store closed."

Hiram shook his head in dismay. "When was this?"

"Before six-thirty, I would guess."

"Sit down, Edward. There is something

that you need to know."

It was nearly ten-thirty and Hiram kept his vigilant watch for Ruthia's return. Zanya and Rufus sat in the kitchen, contemplating the possibilities of Ruthia's absence. Sophia soon joined Hiram.

"Ruthia's not here, yet?"

"Nay," Hiram mumbled and made his eighteenth trip back to the window.

"Oh dear, she may be having car trouble. I will get Rahzvon to drive over there."

"Nay!" Hiram blurted out. He resumed a calming tone, "I can go."

He drove slowly on the dark desolate road toward the old Sierzik residence. There was not another vehicle in sight. He gradually increased his speed; he had a nagging fear that something was very wrong. Maybe she had discovered the contraband hidden in Stan's inventory and feared returning home; after all, she had given him one of the dispensers. She may have been afraid that he had discovered the secret contents, too. Perhaps she was scared that she would be a suspect in the crime. The £4oo from Edward may have been her means to get away.

Hiram removed one hand from the steering wheel and rubbed his forehead now aching with stress. He drove on.

After finding the Sierzik home vacant and

dark, he returned to his estate, anxious and frustrated. Livia, Rahzvon, Sophia, Zanya, and Rufus met him in the main corridor.

"She was not there."

"She can't be in the village. The only place open is the pub and I know that she's not there," Zanya remarked feebly.

Hiram studied the expressions of the concerned parents. It was time to tell them.

"Sophia, Rahzvon, please join Livia and me in my study. Zanya, take Rufus to the kitchen and offer him some refreshment."

Hiram sat facing the shocked, devastated parents. Upon hearing the facts, Rahzvon had instantly gone berserk, ready to take revenge on Seton for endangering his child. Sophia burst into tears and blamed herself for permitting the relationship. Hiram's detailed plan to ship the sisters off to London and to apprehend Seton in their absence did little to comfort Sophia and Rahzvon. Ruthia was missing. Every strike of the grandfather clock voiced a sense of impending doom.

"Rahzvon, she may have taken a room at the inn. You drive there, I will check with the Wheatons, Margret's Row, and with Allison and Adam," Hiram instructed.

Livia led Sophia to the parlor to sit, after the two men left to continue the search.

"Sophia, have faith. Do not think the worst. They will probably be returning with her within the hour. After all, Stanford is not due back for two weeks."

"I wish my mother was here," Sophia sniffled.

"Yes, Hannah is a tower of strength. But you *are* her daughter. You can be strong for your family. I know you can. I'll order some tea."

The two women sat in silence, lost in the details of the situation.

Finally, Livia suggested, "Let's talk about something else. How *is* your mother?"

"I received a letter a few days ago. She wanted to come home for Ruthia's wedd—" she burst out sobbing.

Livia embraced her shoulders. "Now, now...is she still dating Mr. Raheleka?"

Sophia wiped her eyes with a hankie from her dress pocket.

"Yes. She thinks a great deal of him. He is such a nice man—not like that wretched Stenford!"

Livia sighed. "Well. I am thankful that she has someone like Mr. Raheleka after losing Oscar."

"Yes, I never knew Mother to be so upset as the day she received the telegram that he was missing in—oh, Livia, my Ruthia is missing!" she cried, reaching for Livia's hands.

Livia held Sophia's, trying desperately to distract her. "Have you heard anything in the news, lately?" she asked weakly.

Sophia looked up. "You know that they caught that evil kidnapper, Hateman."

"Oh, you mean Hauptmann," Livia gently corrected her.

"Yes. Can you imagine someone taking a mere twenty-month old baby from its nursery window?"

"No; the Lindberghs were devastated."

"And then discovering that their poor baby was—" Sophia began crying again. "*My* poor baby!"

Livia gave up, resigned to the fact that it was going to be a very long night if Ruthia did not soon show up.

Rufus and Zanya sat across from each other at the kitchen table.

"'Tis difficult waitin'."

"Yes, it's awful. Being one of triplets, well, I did not want to say anything to my parents, but I know that there is something very wrong. I sense things about Ruthia and Von when we are not together," she said, looking fearful.

The kitchen telephone's ring interrupted.

Zanya answered it anxiously, "Hello, McDonnally residence."

Rufus watched, as her face grew grave. "Yes. She is missing...We don't know. We have no information, yet...Try not to worry...I will. I promise...I love you, too."

She hung up the telephone. A tear ran down her cheek.

"That's what I was trying to tell you. That was Von. He senses it, too." She bit her bottom lip and sat back down. Rufus reached for her hand and held it.

"I understand that feelin'. Phemie and I are close in the same way."

"It's strange. I feel that she is in pain, but I am not sure that it is physical," she said sadly.

Rufus left his chair to console her with a warm embrace.

Livia heard the clock toll. Another hour ticked away. Neither Hiram, nor Rahzvon had returned. Sophia, under Livia's arm, drifted off, sobbing in her sleep.

Livia studied the furnishings. The parlor was the same as it had been when she had first entered the mansion. Despite Hiram's animosity for his father Geoffrey, Geoffrey's portrait still hung prominently over the fireplace. She thought back. She had asked Hiram why it remained. He had answered quietly, "As a reminder of the kind of man I will not become." Hiram was definitely not like his father and she was glad of it. Hiram was an honorable, loving man. For the most part, Geoffrey had a history of being self-centered with little regard for anyone, including Hiram and Hiram's mother. He was a ruthless businessman and an unfaithful husband. Fortunately, some good became of his indiscretion—sweet, loving Guillaume, Hiram's half-brother.

In the kitchen, Zanya slammed her palms down on the table. "I have to go look for her!"

"But where?" Rufus asked.

"Duncan Ridge. She may have gone there to think. We have gone up there to seek peace, countless times."

"Nay yer not goin'—'tis the middle o' the night. I'll go—ye stay here wit' yer ma. She doesna need anot'er bairn to worry o'er."

"Alright, but take Hunter. He loves to run up there and will waste no time getting there. He knows the location of every rock and crag."

"Verra well, go check on yer ma." She left her chair.

He leaned down and kissed her forehead. She looked up at him in wonder. His hands cupped her shoulders. Abruptly, he leaned over and moved his lips to her startled mouth. She looked to his face, which telegraphed the same shock she was feeling. They stood just inches apart, immobile. Caught in the moment, they stared at one another.

"I...I should go, *Wee One.*" He touched her hand, as he left her and exited through the backdoor.

She looked down at her hand. She touched it where he had. "God speed," she whispered.

***

Zanya was right about Hunter. Once he passed through the pasture gate, he broke into a dead run toward Duncan Ridge, cutting through Naomi and Edward's adjoining estate. Rufus, being an expert horseman, kept his seat as Hunter galloped on, leaping over boulders and crags through the misty moors.

Upon reaching the ridge top, Rufus halted the horse and called out into the darkness.

"Ruthia, Ruthia!"

He listened to his faint echo and then called again. He pushed Hunter forward in a slow trot to the edge of the woods and summoned her, again.

Nothing.

"Ruthia, are ye ou' there? Ruthia, 'tis Rufus—answer me!"

He traversed the ridge, north and south. The visibility was poor; his flashlight beam reflected back.

A half hour later, he took one last look around.

"I guess Zanya's hunch must have been wrong. Let's go home," he murmured to his mount. He pulled to the left on the reins and gave the horse a gentle nudge with his heels, but Hunter did not respond. It raised its head, muzzle up, lips rolled back, turning its head slowly back and forth.

"What's wrong, lad? What do ye smell?"

Rufus tried again to move Hunter forward. Instead, the horse took two steps back and then pulled to the right.

"What are ye doin', lad?"

Hunter started down over the crest of the steep ridge—one step at a time. The large hooves broke them from slipping on the fine rocks.

"Halt, Hunter," Rufus demanded, leaning back in the saddle, trying to maintain his balance.

The horse refused and carefully continued down the hill. "Verra well, lad, ye're in charge. Easy."

The two moved forward, ever so slowly. Every three or four steps, the horse would pause, regaining its balance on all fours. Then the unexpected happened. Hunter bellowed a loud call into the darkness, before continuing.

"What is it?" Rufus held his breath on the heart-stopping ride to the bottom of the ravine.

The beam of light from Rufus's torch fell across the overturned sedan—the McDonnally insignia on the door.

"Ruthia!" he yelled in horror and jumped from the saddle. He crawled down to the wreckage and shone the light in through the broken window.

No passengers.

"Ruthia, Ruthia!"

He turned to the clapping of Hunter's hooves on the rocks. Where was he going? Rufus followed for twenty yards from the car on the opposite side. Hunter stopped moving and lowered his head.

Rufus rushed to the crumpled form. "Dear God, please let her be all right."

"Ruthia?" he said fearfully, noting the horrific blood covering her blouse.

"Rufus?" she said weakly.

"Hold on, lassie. We'll get ye home. Do ye think ye hae any broken bones?"

"I don't think so, but I feel so weak." She then passed out in his arms.

Hunter dropped down to the ground.

"Good lad," Rufus said, carefully lifting Ruthia up into the saddle. He climbed up behind her.

"Go home, Hunter, but easy."

The horse seemed to be well aware of its precious cargo and moved gently down the ravine where the lay of the land fanned out onto the road.

Rufus arrived at McDonnally Manor, just as Ruthia regained consciousness. Dr. Lambert arrived shortly thereafter.

The next morning Rufus returned to the manor to check on Ruthia.

"How is she, mum?" he asked Sophia.

"Thanks to you, she will be fine. Her injuries are minor. Dr. Lambert prescribed bedrest for the next week. Thank you for taking the initiation to find her." She hugged him,

Rufus smiled at her mispronunciation.

"May I please see her?"

"Of course, go on upstairs. She is in her room. You will hear them. Zanya and Ivy are with her."

Rufus entered Ruthia's room. Zanya lit up when he walked through the doorway. So did Ruthia.

"Ye look a lot better than ye did last night," he commented, approaching the bed.

"Oh, pish posh, I look absolutely horrid! Come sit next to me, if you can bear it." She turned to her sister. "Zanya, please take Ivy downstairs for some afters. I'd like a few minutes in private with Rufus."

Ivy charged, "You could have asked me to leave. I am not a child!" She led the way. Zanya hesitated at the doorway and looked back at Rufus.

"Go on Zanya," Ruthia demanded.

Rufus nodded at Zanya, as she followed Ivy out into the hall.

"Rufus, you saved my life." Ruthia reached for his hand. "Thank you."

"'Twas not me—Hunter deserves all the credit. I was just along for the ride," he said, grinning. "He was determined to stay on the ridge until we found ye. He risked his life tryin' to save ye."

She sat up straight. "Rufus, he's just a horse. It was so brave of you to go out into the night to search for me. You cannot imagine how terrified I was. But then, there you were, bringing me back to safety."

"Aye, but it was Zanya's i—"

"Rufus I woke up this morning, reliving last night and all that happened. It was worse than any nightmare. *He* had seemed so loving and sincere and then...that grin...that devilish grin and suddenly, he just leapt from the car."

She lowered her head and went silent. A tear trickled down her cheek. Rufus took her hand.

She looked up at him and confessed, "I have been such a fool in so many ways. I truly enjoyed the days that you and I spent together while...while he was gone that week. I should have known from the start that he wasn't one-tenth the man that you are. You have been so good to me. I think that it was the ride to and from London that convinced me. I was just being so materialistic. I was making a dreadful mistake. I belong with you, Rufus McTavish," she said, beaming.

Zanya stood outside the bedroom door, watching and listening. She could not move. *Rufus and Ruthia.* That *is* what he had wanted. Now, that is what Ruthia wanted, as well. Zanya loved her sister and had prayed for her safety—but that kiss—hers and Rufus's—haunted her. She stared at the floor as a deep feeling of sadness came over her.

Hiram seated at the dining room table with Rahzvon and Edward, put down his cup.

"It was quite a night. To think that all that time we were looking for Ruthia, Seton was sitting comfortably in the Strickland home."

"Scotland Yard should have left him with me for just five minutes!" Rahzvon shoved his chair back from the table.

"Aye, and you would have been going to prison with Seton."

Edward scratched his forehead. "So he's been on the lam for some time."

"Aye, and now, he is saddled with another charge of attempted murder to add to his endless list of crimes: smuggling, drug trafficking, theft, forgery, and tax evasion."

Edward shook his head. "Poor Ruthia, her hopes for love were dashed inside of a few hours."

"When your fiancé leaves you in a running vehicle, headed for a cliff, there's no love lost," Rahzvon disputed.

"Thank God that it didn't catch fire, as dry as this season has been. The automobile would have gone up in flames with all of Duncan Ridge," Edward added.

Hiram shook his head in dismay. "I don't even want to imagine it. I think Seton may have counted on that being the case." He sipped his tea. "How's Naomi taking all of this?"

Edward placed his napkin on the table. "Fairly well, now that the initial shock has worn off. It is not every day that you learn that your nephew is an accomplice to a criminal like Seton. She called her mother. Beatrice said that she knew that it could not be Marvin; he is the apple of her eye. But her grandson, Conrad? She always suspected that he was much like his grandfather Cecil."

"To think that I was concerned about Von being a fashion designer—Conrad's only twenty-two. Such a short life," Rahzvon added.

Edward sat down his cup. "Naomi said that when they hauled Seton and Conrad away, Jeanie flew from the house, shouting that Marvin probably knew about his brother's dealings and did nothing about it. There is no proof that he did. However, Jeanie does not trust Marvin and has moved out to the inn with her sister Martha, who apparently is equally upset about *Conrad's* involvement.

"Sorry to hear about that. Marvin is a fine man." Rahzvon sighed.

Zanya stepped outside of the dining room in time to hear Edward's comment, "The only one that would be happy about Jeanie leaving Marvin, would be Rufus."

Another woman wanting Rufus? What chance would she have competing with Jeanie—his childhood sweetheart and Ruthia—his damsel in distress. Zanya, disheartened, walked to the front door to get some fresh air. She opened it.

"Good morning, Zanya."

Shocked by his presence she mumbled,

"Kade?"

"Yes, me in the flesh."

"We didn't expect you. How did you get here, so quickly?" She looked past his large frame. "Is Von with you?"

"No. The last I heard was that he was attending a fashion show with Miss Clayton in Edinburgh."

"So you haven't heard about Ruthia?"

"*No.*"

"She'll want to tell you herself."

"Is she alright?"

"She's fine, now. I'm certain that she'll be glad to see you."

He stepped closer.

"Zanya, you seem upset," he said gently, placing his arm around her.

She quickly wiped the tears from her cheeks. "No, no. It's all the excitement around here. Ruthia's up in her room—Rufus is visiting," she mumbled. "Go on up."

"Miss Sierzik, I am here to see *you.*"

"Me?"

"Yes, I have been thinking about you, quite often, in fact. You know, I was very impressed with the way that you defended Von. You are a very special woman...in so many ways. Anyway, I wanted to do something special for you."

"For me?"

"Yes, you, Miss Sierzik. As fate would have it...well, I have a surprise for you."

He led her through the door out into the portal. There was a strange car parked in the drive. Confused, she examined the limousine and the man that stepped out of it. Who was he? Why was he here? He was not carrying a package or a gift of any kind. The stranger closed the car door and stood motionless. He was tall and thin. He wore a dark mustache and an elegant suit of clothes.

Kade took Zanya's hand and led her down the drive. They stopped in front of the visitor. Met by his broad smile and kind eyes, she nervously returned a brief smile. Kade put his arm around her shoulders.

"Zanya, this is your grandfather—your mother's father."

"My heart will not forget thee
More than the moaning brine
Forgets the moon when she is set;
That thrilled my brain like wine,"

—James Russell Lowell

Non-fiction Entries in Heated Exchange

The Wall Street Crash of 1929 brought financial ruin and hardship to over 15 million people.

In the 1930s the following were popular for women: a shoulder-length hairstyle, a sparkly hair net called a "snood" (originally nets used to protect the long hair for women working around machinery), applying cosmetics as described, eyelash curlers and false eyelashes which required hours to apply.

Alarm clocks, tractors, and iceboxes were used at this time.

One-pound sterling (currency used in Great Britain) equals about $3.50 in 1932.

Famous actors of 1930s were The Marx Brothers, Ronald Colman, Joan Crawford, Jimmy Durante.

The AGA stove manufactured in Great Britain was a top seller.

Dollhouses and electric trains were popular toys, as well as Mickey and Minnie Mouse cartoons.

Scottish Motor Traction Magazine was read at this time.

American past times, chain stores and the inventions mentioned by character "Mr. Seton" were current in the 1930s.

The Oakland Bay Bridge (Golden Gate) in San Francisco and the Lambreth Bridge in London were constructed at this time.

University of Edinburgh Business School was located in Scotland.

The Good Earth was written by Pearl S. Buck.

The Slang (such as "Mitt me" and "Shake a leg") used by younger generation was accurate for this period.

At this time, thirty-six million automobiles were manufactured.

The Japanese industries were booming and undercutting world prices.

Seton is a Scottish surname.

The facts about Peru, the festival, and the Archbishop's Palace in Lima are true.

Installment plans were prevalent with the aftermath of the depression.

The Midland Hotel was located in St. Pancras, London where work was done to eliminate the slums between the years of 1930 and 1933.

Men wore top hats, white ties, coats with tails and pencil thin mustaches.

The Royal Opera House, the New Shakespeare

and Memorial Theatre were frequented then.

Farewell to Arms is a movie starring Gary Cooper.

The Imperial Airways had a flight from London to Paris.

Women's return to the "very feminine" fashions described, was accurate for this period.

Robert Piguet was a fashion designer known for training Christian Dior and Hubert de Givenchy.

Facts of the Charles Lindbergh baby kidnapping are true.

Elsa Shiaparelli, Madeline Vionnet and Coco Chanel were famous fashion designers at this time.

The Ritz Hotel is located at the fashion center at Place Vendôme in Paris, France.

Poetry Excerpts from the Chapters

1 "Light Shining Out of Darkness" by William Cowper

2 German proverb

3 "A Pause of Thought" by Christina Rossetti

4 "Maude Clare" by Christina Rossetti

5 "The World is Too Much with Us" by William Wordsworth

6 Ukrainian proverb

7 Quote by Benjamin Franklin

8 Quote by Abraham Lincoln

9 Quote by Helen Keller

10 "The Years" by Sara Teasdale

11 Tsonga proverb

12 American proverb

13 Quote by Abraham Lincoln

14 "A Narrow Window" by Florence E. Coates

15 "Windy Nights" by Robert L. Stevenson and "Farewell" by James Russell Lowell

Acknowledgements

British English A to Zed. New York: Facts on File, Inc., 2001.

Chronicle of the 20th Century. New York: Chronicle Publications, 1987.

Elliot, David. Summers Lang Syne: Scotland 1930 to 1959.Falkirk, UK: Falkirk Council Cultural Services, 2005.

Grun, Bernard. The Timetables of History: A Horizontal Linkage of People and Events. New York: Simon and Schuster, 1982.

Guide to Peru. Columbus, OH: Highlights for Children, 1996.

Hender, Ann Clark. Memories O' Mine Growing Up in Scotland 1930-1954. Middletown, DE: Ann Clark, 2013.

Mendelsohn, Ink. "We Were What We Wore." American History Vol 39/8, 1988.

Nivens, Felicia L. Fabulous Fashions of the 1930s. Melrose Park, IL: Lake Book Manufacturing Inc., 2012.

The Hutton Getty Picture Collection 1930s. London: Unique House, 1998.

The Life Series 30's & 40's Britain. UK: Ticktock Publishing Ltd., 1998.

This Fabulous Century Volume III and IV. New York: Time-Life Books, 1969.

Webster's New Explorer Desk Encyclopedia. Springfield, MA: Federal Street Press, 2003.

I am a firm believer that education
should be an ongoing endeavor.
I stand by the unwritten law that education
should be entertaining for young and old, alike.
Thus, I incorporate
historic places, people, and events in my novels,
for your learning pleasure.

With loving thoughts,
Arianna Snow

To order copies
of the
Lochmoor Glen Series
and the
Beyond Lochmoor Glen Series

Visit the
Golden Horse Ltd.
website:
www.ariannaghnovels.com

Watch for the second volume
in the series!